OPEN CONCEPT

STORIES

Zachary Amendt

MONTAG

Montag Press
ISBN: 978-1-940233-46-8
Cover art © Piers Chapman
Jacket design – Niall Gray
Editor & Managing Director – Charlie Franco

A Montag Press Book
www.montagpress.com
Montag Press
1066 47th Ave. Unit #9
Oakland CA 94601 USA

Montag Press, the burning book with the hatchet cover, the skewed word mark and the portrayal of the long-suffering fireman mascot are trademarks of Montag Press.

Printed & Digitally Originated in the United States of America
10 9 8 7 6 5 4 3 2 1

"[B]eautifully-written, expertly-paced, and transportive .... a seemingly effortless piece of writing."

— *Defiant Scribe*

"Amendt's strong characterization blends line-by-line with his punchy, inventive sentences to craft an outstanding collection that achieves the dramatic without the melodramatic."

— *The Masters Review*

"I have no doubt that [Amendt's] writing will soon appear in the "Best American NonRequired Reading" anthology or in the Pushcart Prize anthology. I also won't be surprised to hear his name mentioned for any of the prestigious book awards. His writing deserves it."

— Cetywa Powell, Publisher, *Underground Voices*'

For G.L.0

No Love Lost

Caroline waved as Troy stepped off the 574 bus from Tacoma. She wore a maroon t-shirt that read *Goal Digger* and had a zip-up sweater tied around her waist. It was mid-March. Daylight Savings had just begun, but the clock tower at the King Street Station was still an hour behind.

"Suede," she said, toeing his cowboy boots with her galoshes. "And with rain in the forecast."

"Suede," he said, hugging her. "It can't rain on us now, can it?"

It didn't and it wouldn't. It wouldn't dare rain. Troy was relatively new to the Northwest. Strangely, the air felt fresher to him before a downpour than after one. He had never been around so little sun or such rabid sports fans. Also, the traffic was bad.

They walked arm-in-arm to PJ's on Division, one of Seattle's oldest bars, just two blocks from Bill Speidel's Underground Tour.

"I can't believe you're here!" Caroline said. "I'm honored. Is the city what you imagined?"

Troy picked a cherry blossom out of her hair.

"I thought there'd be more tourists," he said.

He had met Caroline seven years before, since right after his engagement to Paige. They were all living in Westchester, N.Y., at the time. He attended a wedding – without Paige as a plus-one – on Caroline's family estate in Pleasantville. During the reception and despite his ineligibility Troy caught the garter while

Caroline snatched the bouquet. She did not accidentally kiss him goodbye that night.

"You look terrific," he said, as a bouncer checked his ID and casually waved her in. "You look fresh."

"Troy," she began "I write briefs, I run 5Ks. But lately I feel like I can't write another word, or take another step."

PJ's reminded him of the cocktail bars in Manhattan he had frequented in his twenties. It was Caroline's favorite place in Seattle. She took all her suitors here, and even had most the songs memorized on the jukebox by their letters and numbers. *Lush Life* was D12. *Rhiannon*, A1.

"Dad took me here on my 21st ," Caroline said. "This table is very significant to me. I had my very first sip here. Right *here*."

She laid her caressing palms on its surface.

"You should have carved your initials into it when you had the chance," Troy said.

The ceilings were decorative tin and the exposed brick walls soaked up most of the sunlight. On the menu were cocktails named Happy Pinecone, An Apple a Day, Harkonen.

"So, how's the wifey?"

"That's a good question."

"You don't know?"

Paige had traveled to upstate New York for a reunion. Her family had rented a cabin next to a Hasidic Jewish summer camp, chiefly because it had no cellular reception.

"I'd like to meet her one of these days," Caroline said.

"You'd love her," Troy said. "You'd be fast friends."

He caught Caroline catching glances of herself in the mirror behind him. She was finishing up law school at Seattle Pacific, poring over woefully long texts and international statutes that sounded like German submarines from WWII.

"As a 3L and co-editor of the law review," she said, "I have to organize the 'Hundred Days' party, which is weird because it's 87 days to graduation, and 130 to the Bar Exam, and our professors don't call it an exam. It's a *quiz*. Ha!"

She laughed as if she were being tickled.

"Maybe they'll draw a smiley face near the score when they hand it back," Troy said.

Every lawyer he knew did not practice law. One did standup comedy. Another taught yoga.

"I'm only laughing because I can't cry anymore," she said. "It's no cakewalk. I don't even know what day it is. I'm hanging on by the skin of my skin."

"At least you have that to hold onto," Troy said.

"And this," Caroline said, hoisting her coupe. "Thank God for alcohol."

She thought she drank heavily, but she didn't know. She had no idea what heavy was.

"Hangovers used to be a little easier on us, remember?"

"I was never that young," Troy said.

"You were famous for it. How old are you now? 33, 35?"

He nodded.

"I'm thirty," she said, as if it was far away. "Adulthood isn't exactly turning out as I had hoped."

She let out a sigh, almost inaudible. Her exhale nearly scalded him. He wanted to tell her that the unpleasantness wasn't behind her, but ahead. That there was no time unless she wrested it from the time she'd already wasted, loitering in school, waiting for things to happen.

"Let's close out here," she said. "I want to show you around town."

She excused herself to the john while Troy carefully inspected and paid the bill. They walked out of PJ's holding hands. The skyscrapers were shiny. Seattle felt fresh but used.

"Don't tell anyone," Caroline whispered, "but I got you a little souvenir."

She removed a small vial from her purse. It was a pepper shaker from PJ's.

"You shouldn't have," he joked.

"I steal hearts, too," she said.

Troy kissed her right then. He couldn't help it. It was as if their lips were grafted together. He knew she liked her hair pulled. She tasted like flavorless chapstick and spearmint, faintly.

"This is why I'm never without gum," she said afterwards, taking a breath. "And you're like a human furnace in that jacket. Aren't you warm? What are you hiding under there?"

Troy only had on short-sleeves underneath. He recoiled when Caroline reached in and unbuttoned his shirt.

"I want to see," she insisted.

"I don't know. I'm a little deeper-chested these days," he said.

"So am I. Five pounds." Caroline adjusted her bra, clasped in the front. "All of it went right *here*."

Her heart lived under there, somewhere. After a breezy tour of Pike's Place – past Beecher's cheese shop, the Gum Wall, the very first Starbucks – she led Troy to a wine bar with an outside patio and a shuffleboard court, seemingly ideal for legitimate rendezvous, like business lunches, or first dates.

"Damn the Weather," Caroline said. "Surpassing blends. And, four stars on Yelp."

"I must take Paige here," Troy said.

They selected a carafe of the house cab. Several tables over and within earshot, an elderly couple dined on charcuterie with menus resting on their walkers, eating slowly, more silent than the *p* in psoriasis.

"To us," Caroline raised her glass, garishly. "To the new yuppies."

They were in luck: they had caught some late sunshine. In it, Caroline's earrings glinted and swung like tiny chandeliers. They did not look expensive – a pair of unpolished spiral loops

– but Troy didn't know much about jewelry. Paige's ears were unpierced. She preferred flowers.

"May I?" Troy asked.

He touched her earlobes. The hoops spun. Caroline winced.

"Dad got these for me when I left high school. I know they're not pretty, but I'm sentimental, obviously."

"How are you holding up?"

"I think about him every day," she said. "They told me he died doing what he loved. I don't think they say that to Army families."

"You never told me how it happened."

"Osprey," she said. "Clipped the deck of an aircraft carrier. And … yeah. Pretty quick. Last week the investigators asked if I wanted to listen to his cockpit recorder."

"Did you?"

"I couldn't. What if he was scared?" She emptied her glass, down to the lees. "What if his last words weren't words?"

"I can empathize," Troy said.

"Should we order another carafe?" Her tongue was the color of plum. "Wine is essential for anyone who's lost a parent."

"Or two," Troy said.

"I forgot. Oh, I'm sorry." She bit her lip. "You are a special case."

It was unfair of him to say it in the first place. Caroline had so much going on in her life, too much to hear the boring details about Perry's and Kathleen's car accident and the trip Troy made to Jack London's gravesite in Glen Ellen with their remains. They used to read *The Call of the Wild* to him at bedtime and Troy wanted other people making the pilgrimage to the great man's gravesite – not a grave so much as a hunk of granite at the end of a footpath, a sorcerer's stone – to also, unknowingly, make a pilgrimage to his parents' place of rest. It was 112 degrees the day he deposited their ashes; Troy was more afraid of the rattlesnakes than of getting caught. He didn't see Caroline often enough for her to know things this intimate, like the fact that Perry and Kathleen were safe people who had died with their seat belts on, after a family dinner where they joked about drunk driving. Or, that their marriage was like a book so old that every page fell out as you turned it. Caroline didn't deserve that part of him that he would otherwise save for Paige, when she was around. His wife.

"I was just thinking," Troy said.

"Yes?"

"We've only seen each other seven times, total."

Caroline was skeptical. He listed them. Eighteen holes at Bethpage Black. Ping-pong on the rooftop of the Standard Hotel in the West Village. Three headliners at Coachella Music Fest. The somnolent wine train along the Finger Lakes. The night at the Hotel del Coronado when she said if a couple stared into one other's eyes for four minutes it was love, and they didn't last forty seconds before room service arrived. Her friend's wedding.

"And this," Troy said, taking her hand in his, until she withdrew it.

"Do you feel guilty?"

"No."

"Do you think Paige has a lover?"

"It's not in her character," he said. "I imagine a married woman has to flirt twice as hard."

Marrying Paige had been like buying a refurbished refrigerator. It was serviceable. No warranty.

"But you love her."

"I do love her."

"And it's a life sentence."

"And I'm happy," Troy said.

"And happily married people have affairs."

In the strongest of passions, there is neither respite nor mercy. Caroline had a narcotic effect on him. She had made his life more elastic. At 16 her father had let her drive cross country, by herself, because he wanted her to know that the world was safe for adventure. Whereas Troy had grown up afraid. He was raised on and by fear. Every drop of rain was acid rain. Every fly was the Medfly. Every meadow meant Lyme disease.

By 6:30 p.m. the outdoor tables began to fill. A waiter edged by and Troy signed his name in the air instead of asking for the check. He paid this time with cash, with crisp bills he kept in a leather billfold, his father's name embroidered inside, in gold leaf. Perry had kept everything in it: receipts, newspaper cartoon clippings, bet slips on longshot ponies from the old Hollywood Park. He showed these to Caroline, explaining what a $2 win meant, what a boxed trifecta involved, who *Sally Forth* was.

"Could these be winning horses?" she asked, smoothing out the wrinkles in the slips.

"Doesn't matter," he said. "They're expired."

When the change arrived it blew off the table, onto Caroline's feet. She bent down and put it in her pocket.

"Thank you," she said.

"You need money?"

"Always."

"I thought there had been a settlement."

Caroline hung her head.

"The lawyers all got it," she said.

"I wish I had met him."

"Didn't you meet Dad at my place, when we first met?"

"He was deployed," Troy said.

"Naturally," she said. "He'd have liked you."

"Think so?"

She emptied her purse out on the table to prove it. In among her tampons and stain removers was a small, framed photo of a flier in a scarf and chunky shoe-black eyeglasses that made his face look craggy. His name was Bruce; he was Irish; she had gotten his looks. *Irish babies cry with a brogue*, he told her later, and he made sure to fill the family scrapbooks so she had a sense of who she was and where she came from. There were, in contrast, so few pictures of Perry and Kathleen. Troy didn't know who he looked more like, who he took after. He knew that he was supposed to have a brother, and that when describing the miscarriage his father simply told him: *The stork flies over but it does not always deliver.* He knew that their lives were measured by milestones and paychecks. That they took short vacations together: weekends in Reno, last-minute cruises out of Galveston, yearning to misbehave, but tamely. He wished they were still around, just so he could get them on the phone, just once, not to tell them he loved them – they knew that already – so much as to ask them how they made their vows work until death. Because he wanted to break his and Paige's, almost on a nightly basis.

They headed back toward the waterfront. Caroline was in the middle of recalling a funny childhood memory when she interrupted herself.

"Oh, no."

"What?"

"My earrings," she said.

One had fallen out somehow. Caroline insisted on retracing their steps. She looked in every vestibule, asked each bartender, scoured every Lost and Found. Troy had never seen such fruitless tenacity, but he scanned the sidewalks with her for what felt like hours, crouched in the gutters, scouring the bushes, accosting strangers, until she sat down on a bench in Pioneer Square to rest.

"It's like losing Dad all over again," she said.

Troy wanted to remind her that she had a large piece of him still: The Black Box. There hadn't been one in his parents' Prius.

"I'm so sorry," he said. "What can I do?"

"I don't know." Her shoulders dropped. "Ice cream sounds good right about now."

They both yawned, as if it were contagious. Troy checked his watch.

"8:55. The last bus is in 20 minutes. I should go."

"No," she said.

"I really should."

"Just come home with me."

All night Troy felt like he was playing catch with an auto-graphed baseball.

"Are you sure?" he said.

"Might as well," she shrugged.

She lived with her mother in Queen Anne. They called for a car.

"Here's the thing," Caroline said in the Uber. "Mom's awake, she knows you're married. You'll have to climb up the back wall."

"Okay."

"Unless you want to sleep on the couch."

"I'm fine," he said.

"A wall," she said. "Not a fence."

The driver's route brushed up against the Space Needle. It was not a city Troy could imagine or recognize. New York made him want to eat life; Chicago, drink it; Los Angeles, film it. Seattle made him take it for granted. It's what made the Northwest an excellent choice: there was nowhere else to go. He and Paige had lived in or vetoed every other city, even those they'd never been to, sight unseen. Seattle was the greenhouse without windows they had been looking for, the snow globe without snow.

"She wants to settle down here," Troy said.

"Is that why you're here? Scouting the joint?" Caroline smacked her lips. "Good job, Paige. How do you get there?"

"Where? Five years of marriage?"

Troy didn't know the answer himself. Happy spouses share top billing. Paige was quite a woman, redoubtable in her opin-ions, more complex than nuclear fission. Troy could have defended her. There was a lot to defend. Her morality wasn't situational, like his. Infidelity was more taboo for Paige than blackface, and she had one of those last names – Plog – that other girls got married to get rid of. But she kept hers. She wouldn't buckle.

"Driver, I have a problem with this," Caroline said as the car pulled to a stop.

The fare was higher than they had been quoted. It was because she had selected a larger vehicle, an SUV instead of a Towncar. Still, she talked it down.

"I almost forgot I'm a lawyer," she said.

Troy unbuckled her belt, and then his.

"You have to pass the quiz first," he said.

Her mother's townhouse was part of a newer tract with a view of Puget Sound. The streets were lined with oleanders, eucalyptus, an Eden of invasive species. The motion detectors were sensitive and Troy could see Caroline watching from inside her room as he went around back – past the *Beware of Dog* and *Trespassers Will Be Composted* caution signs – and surveyed the six-foot cinderblock wall protecting her from guys like him, trying to find a foothold.

It took him a minute to scramble up. She gave him a golf-clap as he leapt down from the sill.

"Not a fence," he said, huffing.

"Told you," she said.

Her bedroom was decorated in chiffon and Monet. They were close enough to ignite each other. Her nightgown was so lovely, he nearly tore it to shreds. She had the complexion of a Jordan almond. He found a dead butterfly tattooed on the small of her back. She pivoted, to show him everything, her every angle.

"Your turn," she said.

Troy removed his belt. He didn't have to unbutton his shirt to show her the popsicle-red medallions covering his forearms, welts of all sizes, small as colibri, nebulous as a bruise. It was dry skin. It was genetic. It wasn't contagious, he said. But Caroline looked as if she had smashed open a piggy bank and found nothing inside.

"Please," Troy said. "I'm incarcerated inside this body."

He rubbed his forearms, child-like, as if touching them would make the eczema go away.

"Let's just go to bed," she said.

He turned off the light so Caroline wouldn't have to look at it. He explained how he had tried to overcome it with every steroid imaginable, and how it had migrated, like he had, west and then north, from his legs up to his torso.

"It's a shame," she said.

They slept. Her snoring woke him up several times. At 6 a.m. she wiped her eyes, pulled back the covers and leapt out.

"Hiking trip," she said. "In Bellingham. I totally forgot."

Troy dressed as she put on her makeup. He left the way he came in. The wall seemed to have grown ten feet overnight. He hoped her memory of the evening would dissolve, like an antacid tablet, or that she'd forgive him for his corrupt skin and for opening and closing his marriage whenever he wanted to. Two months later, as an apology and with congratulations, he mailed Caroline a graduation gift (his invitation to her Hundred Days party hadn't arrived in the mail, for some reason): a copper bangle in the shape of a feather that she would never wear because the metal turned her flesh green.

Who is Pilar Furlong?

Pilar only started hearing mosquitoes at a certain time of night. It was not a paper moon outside but a paper *mâché* moon, pasted onto the evening, tinged with bluish watercolors, half of it torn off. She wished the moon and her mood were another color. This part of Redwood City ("Climate Best by Government Test!") was a hard neighborhood for a recluse, its many solicitors and proselytizers and kids selling chocolate bars to fundraise for their little league uniforms, because the new Ferrari dealership across the street – she had watched the well-dressed salesmen, all that afternoon it seemed, paint a fire hydrant red, white, and green – didn't have the decency to sponsor the local tee-ball teams. Everything was either beginning or ending for Pilar, and none of what was happening had the decency to consult or ask her first, for her okay or veto. For instance, her favorite radio station, Be-Bop 92, was shutting down in a few days, its license having been sold to a conglomerate that had no interest in preserving jazz; quietly the disc-jockeys had gone deeper into the vaults, sublimating their lamentations through songs Pilar used to recognize – *Confirmation, Swinging with Symphony Sid, Au Privave* – until life accelerated and swiftly and deftly robbed her of her discerning, if at times tone-deaf, ear. She also loved puns.

It was the things she loved that she tended to drift away from. She could hear Dave in the other room, the bathroom, humming as he shaved, his decade-old beard trimmer sputtering, on its last legs. She pressed hard at her temples. It was a new thing to her, these headaches. They started when Dave took on extra hours at Laconañda, the fifth restaurant in the South Bay to receive its very first Michelin star (though the tilde rendered its name virtually unpronounceable to most of its patrons). Dave, a third-generation graduate of Saint Thomas Aquinas High School, chiefly credited God for this success, and he began tithing more at church on Sunday mornings, except in the fall when his favorite football teams had 10 a.m. kickoffs (Pacific Time). Alongside and exacerbating the headaches, Pilar had felt more colicky and combustible lately, an overall impatience and shortness with Dave; she couldn't pinpoint exactly why. She had been so excited at first for his dramatic career change – from car mechanic to maître-D, from grease monkey to monkey suit – that she began to organize her life completely around food, joining him as he lugged home and scarfed down gourmet leftovers, watching her reactions to the innovative fare he saved for her in brown recyclable containers (themselves made from previously recycled, unsoiled to-go boxes), as proud as a line cook who expected a standing ovation for his amuse-bouche.

"What time is it?" Dave yelled from the john.

"Almost ten."

"Time for bed," he said.

"I suppoths," she lisped.

Pilar was wearing a mouthpiece to straighten her bottom row of teeth, which were not unsightly, but crooked enough to cut her lip at times. Like a retainer, or dentures, it gave her a slight speech impediment. She heard that this treatment would not only cut down on her snacking, it would help her stop biting her nails, which she did not out of nervousness usually, but to forget her hunger.

"Please turn off the water while you're shaving," she yelled.

"Almost done."

"We have to conserve."

"I'm doing my part," he said.

"Your long showers are really irrigating me."

"I drought it," Dave replied.

He emerged from the bathroom with a bit of shaving cream affixed to his chin, surprised to see Pilar in lingerie that was so old and used that it seemed to wilt on her. Her face was full; her waistline, a séance. Her diet had not been going well. She was oscillating between low-calorie, low-carb frozen meals and serious fattening relapses she attributed to being a night owl, though the midnight oil, she soon found out, does not always burn. Whenever Dave looked at her like this – she had noticed this face of his more and more recently – she felt she wasn't a woman to him but instead something to keep him warm at night, like an electric blanket, or a hot water bottle.

Winter was waning, but still chilly. They had agreed all that season to warm the house with ceramic space heaters – metallic, scorching, expensive air – because they didn't know how to fix the flue in the fireplace. Not even their landlord knew how.

"The air's hot," Dave said.

She opened the sliding patio door, and the neighborhood cat waltzed inside. Engraved on its collar – nameless, like the cat in Breakfast at Tiffany's – was a phone number that was out of service (Pilar had tried calling three times). A snort of catnip and a treat, and he went merrily on his way.

"I don't know why you let him in," Dave said.

"He lets himself in."

"You're making him dependent on us."

"I see someone shivering, I want to fix it, not just throw a blanket over it."

The cat bit Dave once, on the hand. He panicked and, afraid of rabies, drove himself to the emergency room. "Feral cat lover," he sneered at Pilar, though the on-duty RNs said the wound was cleaner than most dog bites they saw. Dave really was – and Pilar knew this was true the majority of the time, albeit a slim majority – an effervescent sweetheart under all of his barnacles, a young man with a hankering for love and all of the malcontents it brings. When they were courting he carved their initials into every tree and table he could find. She couldn't find that boy in this man anymore ... his priorities or the tempo of his dreams had changed, or their paths and visions no longer dovetailed, yet tonight (as with most nights) she found herself caressing him when she should have socked him. Dave recoiled politely from her touch, muttered "Too tired," and pulled back the covers.

"Get in," he added.

"No."

"Another all-nighter?"

Pilar felt her gums swelling.

"Yeth, a writing test," she said.

"What's the gig?"

She fluffed up his pillow and lay next to him, on top of the covers, popping her teeth out as if she were about to eat.

"It pays well," she said. "A dollar a word."

"You never answer me directly. You always answer the question you *wish* you were asked."

"I'm writing some questions for a few episodes of Jeopardy," she said.

"You mean, you're writing the answers," Dave said.

For such an emotional cripple, she thought, he did have amazing intellectual dexterity.

"Do you really have to sleep so soon?" she entreated, playfully prodding him in the ribs, tickling him under the sheets. "Can't I talk to you?"

"It's so late, Pilar."

"Just talk."

"About?"

"You know very well what."

She tried to explain it to him: A child takes an interest in her father's life, dismayed that there is not only no biography available but no record he existed at all. And then a flood of memories that hadn't lost any of their edge or danger. She suddenly remembered being 5 years old and stepping on all of the cracks in the sidewalk when she was upset at him, knowing she'd never actually break his back, until the day he slipped a disc in his neck and she blamed herself for walking so maliciously. It was the same with the memories she blocked out in junior high school, when she broke her left leg on purpose – leaping from a treehouse, she recalled – primarily to get out of gym class, but also for the promised painkillers.

"I thought you're seeing a shrink so we don't have to keep talking like this," Dave said.

"Maybe my wounds take longer to heal."

It wasn't the wounds that made her cringe, but the scars.

"You're always like this before bedtime …"

"You treat it like it's my fault that I don't have any parents."

"You have his number now!" Dave said. "Call him!"

She didn't ask Dave to track down her father. He got the information for her as a birthday gift from a lineage-tracing company that specialized in long-lost reunions, and (according to the advertising collaterals) "*grafting new boughs onto barren family trees.*"

"And say what?"

"Say hello, chew him out, you're a jerk, I don't know. I paid good money for those digits. Can I sleep now?"

Every woman needed a room of her own, and every man a kitchen of his own. It was, indeed, a nice gesture and a pretty penny. Dave had been a talented but precariously employed mechanic when the economy went south and bottomed out, like bad weather. *You're young,* they told him, *you'll land on your feet,* as if he had another choice. So he overhauled his application collaterals, added a 'Proficiencies' section to his resume (*"Polite, prompt, willing to pay my dues and roll up my sleeves ..."*) and paid a graduate student from San Jose State $70 to edit his cover letter. And voila! A job on the salad station of a brand new eatery materialized. Laconañda's interior had been just been remodeled to look like Rick's Café American in *Casablanca*. The piano player knew Charlie Haden and Johnny Hartman standards by heart. "Who's this Rick?" Dave had asked her the day of his hiring.

"What if I'm scared to call him?" Pilar asked.

"He can't hurt you."

"I guess you're not scared of anything."

Dave grunted and flipped over onto his stomach.

"Not much," he said into his pillow.

"So, what are you most afraid of?"

"Skin cancer," he said.

She laughed, convulsively.

"You're not?"

"I thought you'd say nuclear winter, deforestation ..."

"Oh," he said. "Those too."

2:13 a.m.

There was nothing else an insomniac could do. Pilar did her best work nocturnally, splattering herself on every answer, plagiarizing from obscure sources. Home was not exactly the most inspiring environment. She spent most of the night trying to find what to watch on TV, and usually settled on an American cooking contest, where the chefs put their hands up after the time expired as if they had just committed a crime.

This film won the Academy Award for Best Picture
in 1943 – the same year Citizen Kane was released.

Call him. That fertile, impossible idea. She knew her father was Italian, Borgia blood, which made her part-royalty.

*William Shakespeare died on the same day – August 4, 1604 – as
this Spanish writer, known as the 'Man from La Mancha.'*

At thirteen, when he abandoned her to foster care, she was
the underdog in dire need of orthodontia, tearing up her baby
photos – what few she had – because she believed she was ugly
in them.

*The life and reputation of this Caribbean orphan and
American founding father – interred at Trinity Church on Wall Street –
has been reimagined in this eponymous Tony-award winning musical.*

Up all night. Neither an early bird nor a night owl be. Turns
out that at one dollar a word, contractions don't pay.

4:56 a.m.

She woke Dave up because she was scared and she needed him to
understand what she couldn't talk to her analyst about.

"What is *How Green Was My Valley?* Who is Cervantes?
Who is Hamilton?" she asked, really wanting to know.

Not just that, though, but how she liked going to the beach
on rainy days, the desert in the summertime, and ski resorts during
snowmelt. That she loved the smell of gasoline and felt pens. How
she enjoyed opening other people's mail. She missed being 20, thin
and tan. The superficial stuff. As she talked she could tell Dave was
not much interested, and maybe even still asleep, though he gave
her all of the good listening cues, like eye contact, and nodding,
and licking his lips, and checking the back-lit digital clock on the
nightstand as she delved into a complicated and painful past, a har-
rowing house that was impossible to haunt because – like the rou-
lette of foster homes she had gone through – there were too many
people living there. Her past was the woman who was impressed
that her boyfriend had her number memorized; the boy who said
that he inherited a Mont Blanc from his grandfather when in fact

he stole it from the estate of his cousin who was into calligraphy; the known molester who caught the bride's garter; the graduate instructor who, lacking the money for *It's a Boy* cigars when his son was born, handed out granola bars; the 24-hour gym that's closed from midnight to 4 a.m.; the children for whom going swimming counts as bathing; the DDS who refuses to fix the typo in his shingle: *Denistry*; the French restaurant closed on V-Day because of a surprise health inspection; the executive who doesn't know that he can't afford to put off that haircut for much longer; the actor who starts every morning with a carafe of OJ and a tin of sardines; the golfer with the undiagnosed fear of eating on the course, his food tumbling onto the pesticide-drenched greens; the atheistic realtor who goes to church to boost his clientele; the mogul who disinherited his youngest daughter for no apparent reason; the cocktail waitress who doesn't mind being objectified, and even anticipates it some hours; the monkeys on her chest; the tremble in the custard; the physicist who found the formula for love was time and other variables; the snowboarder who breaks his femur every November, without fail; the 13-year-old boy capable of driving a big rig; the shy man who dreams of circumnavigating the globe in a kayak; the tycoon who bought the town's armory just to install and shoot hoops in; the fashionista who wants to move to New York so terribly that she can't bear the mention of Manhattan; the exotic dancer kicked out of her apartment for breeding lemurs; the dignitary who doesn't know his fly is open; the biker who actually met his wife while he was standing on the corner in Winslow, Arizona; the lady with the fool's gold eye; the tears thick as Karo syrup; the calm before the calm.

Dave murmured "Mmm-hmm," and fell back onto his pillow.

7:15 a.m.

Dave's alarm went off, as loud as a bullhorn. Getting up this easily and early was nasty business. He claimed to be a morning person, which he was not. Still, Pilar envied him, his passing the day making money, restless, fitfully sleepless, and yet waking up late, inexplicably, implacably, idiot-happy.

"What's for breakfast?" he asked. It was the only meal she knew how to make.

"Diet shake for me, eggs and pork chops for you."

"Grilled?"

"Breaded."

"Dreaded pork again," he said.

Shake n' Bake breakfast, getting cold. She poured herself a date smoothie as Dave stirred his French press.

"Wait," she said.

"Are you saying grace?"

"No, I have to pop out my teeuf."

She was on the 9th of 15 sets of the new orthodontia. Her gums were constantly sore.

"How's your diet going?"

"Heinous. I'm over it." she said.

"If you want to look 25 again ..."

There's verbal violence you don't even have to raise your voice for. Dave was one of the last good immoral men. Insensitive, barbaric, and more concerned with the quantity and not the quality of his pushups. When he told her "the house doesn't need cleaning, it needs exorcising," she intuited that he didn't mean a priest, but a treadmill.

"Carrying a little extra weight, so what? I know, I know," Pilar said. "I was fit and beautiful. I will be again." She pulled her hair back into a bun. "Or do I sound too much like the faded starlet in *Sunset Boulevard*?"

Dave leaned across the table and kissed her, more out of reassurance than pity. The gesture startled her.

"In 2002," he said, re-applying his lip balm, "these very lips kissed this Polish pontiff's hand at the Vatican."

"Who is Benedict?" she said.

"Who is John Paul?" he corrected.

"I love you," she said.

"I know."

"Lest the quotidian ever asphyxiate my endearments."

She didn't know, when she learned those words, how often she would use them. She used a lot of words Dave didn't know. He was more of a numbers guy.

"I know you do," he repeated.

"What are your hopes and dreams today?"

"One of our sous chefs is leaving."

"I'm sorry."

"Turnover is the nature of the beast," he shrugged.

He was eating his pork chop not with the silverware Pilar had arranged on a fancy napkin (at 6 a.m., she might have added, at the crescendo of his snoring) but with his fingers, plucking the bread crumbs from off the meat (egg whites making an excellent binder).

"Have you ever thought that you might be the beast?" she asked.

Faintly Pilar heard a familiar scatology, coming from the radio. Be-Bop 92 had all but suspended their six-month-long pledge drive for survival. It was just beautiful, uninterrupted commercial-less noise now.

"Ella," she said.

"What?"

"*Mack the Knife*. This is Ella Fitzgerald, with Louis Armstrong."

Dave continued eating, wordlessly.

"Satchmo," she continued. "When he started in on the horn, Ella plum forgot the lyrics. So she made up her own."

"Sounds terrible," Dave said with his mouth full.

"They gave her a Grammy for it."

As if something had hit him, Dave inspected the remnants

of her blender – dates, bananas, a smidge of honey, powderized protein – and poured her a second shake up to around the midway point of her glass.

"I've already had my breakfast," she said.

"This is the problem," he said. "Let's do a small experiment. Is your glass half full or half empty?"

She looked at the coagulated, cold, vitamin-laden, purple mess she was relegated to eating every morning, in lieu of real, actual food.

"Neither," she said.

"It's one or the other."

"You can't fill a glass halfway and ask me to pick sides!"

"Please go see your analyst," he said. "I'm begging you."

"I thought that's what a live-in boyfriend was for," she said. "Free therapy."

A half-hour later Dave pinched her belly and gathered up his chef's knives. Standing in the doorway (Cat bolting in, sprinting under the couch) he blew her one of his patented, divine goodbye kisses, and Pilar – fatigued by the 3 and 4 a.m. noises that could have been rats, or ghosts, or burglars, or just her imagination – realized that she had not tried hard enough, or indeed ever, to catch one of these kisses in mid-air. That there were entire months' worth of kisses just floating there, orbiting their living room. So for the first time, she closed her eyes and jumped, and, confident she had caught one, ran into the front yard as he unlocked his Subaru to finally prove to him, firmly holding onto her fistful of air before retreating into the kitchen and sealing it up in a Mason jar, that she could – she really *could* – if she tried. See?

Ecstatic Gringo

Hamtramck, its roads pocked, its lots upended. Everyone's underwater. But there's the rumor of urban renewal, a new casino, a smattering of food trucks converging, and a feeling that recovery is possible, and that what it comes down to is miles per gallon.

The Detroit Metro is perfect if location doesn't matter to you, as it doesn't to me. I take a back room in the split-level home of an ex-autoworker and his comatose wife. The garage is his province and domain. Now that the government's making cars, we're all part-owners of the manufacturer that laid this Mel Sloper and the 200,000 others off last year.

Off the line, chewing fat is Mel's new pastime. There are two folding chairs in the Slopers' garage; in between them is a Hills Bros. coffee tin into which we men spit our Skoal. It's in the detritus of decades of hoarding, pack-ratting – busted bulbs, decayed cardboard, the floor caked in antifreeze. He has built hot-rods here, rebuilt engines. Sloper's heart works on the same principles of a piston engine: reliable, if cared for. If not, erratic, temperamental. For most of his life it was quiescent; he joined the union; he did not roil his superiors. Working under the hoods rested him.

Much as he likes talking about it, a lot of our conversations are Mel monologuing and me listening without any mechanical acumen. His tools are as foreign to me as astrolabes. But he knows I know a thing or two about music.

"You know of any place I can sell my records?" he asked. He has boxes and boxes of vinyl, pristinely conditioned, although he has migrated to CDs.

I told him I could sniff out vinyl just about anywhere, in any neighborhood, you name it.

"Raleigh's buys records," I said. "Down on Eight Mile."

Eight Mile, which reminded him of drive-in movies and a thinner, less catatonic wife, reminded me of Eminem. This decrepit city photographs lovely. It has a photogenic memory of things past. The old ballpark. The Edsel.

"Maybe I just should give them to my niece."

"Don't," I said. "Becca's daughter? She'll use them as Frisbees and frame the covers on her wall."

The daily plummeting of our city's currency is slapstick comedy. Detroit's not unlike all the Chair Force cities that staggered along for a while, whirring unconsciously until the bases were shuttered: the servicemen cast out, unaided, into the private sector: and we once again prevailed upon the modern ghost town. Last year, dreadful last year, we all fell down yet again, but things are better now, two-thousand-ten, a new decade: more resigned, our expectations less, and there is finally some money in the mattress, and folks are gardening more, though the soil is dense with lead, growing their own food, composting.

In the 1980s the Slopers were sold/suckered into vinyl siding (more lead) and Astroturf for the lawn. They first plastered their surname on the mailbox and the welcome mats. His wife hung a sign in the window: *Avon Sold Here. Eloise Sloper, Agent.* She was good at cosmetics and addicted to General Hospital.

Mel said, "Eloise isn't much to look at, but she's got great big tits."

I scratched my beard. The fireflies were out tonight, and bothersome. I was losing focus in the flash-outs.

"I always wanted a woman with great big tits," he said. In case there was any deficit in my understanding.

Since its takeover Mel's old corporation's gone through several iterations of bankruptcy – Chapter 11, Chapter 22 – never has our faith in government been so completely and swiftly shaken – and Mel, he was no sunshine patriot. He has talked of starting a community council, simply titled *48212*. When he gets righteous on politics it's hard to stop him. The object of his ire is often the man at the top.

"Obama's a starfucker," Mel said.

I didn't disagree, but the liberals were financing my fellowship.

"Say more about that, Mel."

The night he was shitcanned Mel got fully whisked and we drove into Grosse Pointe to stomp on the hoods of the rich folks' Jaguars and Audis. He was in fatigues and loud, setting off alarms and motion detectors, what a sight. He didn't know those cars weren't made overseas.

"All over the tabloids and doing interviews in cooking magazines. It's not fair," he said, lifting his hand up to the waning light, "what we did to McCain."

I said, "Listen to you. *Mel*odrama."

"Seven years in a POW camp should have counted for something."

Mel thinks, because the numbers are even, that this year will turn out his way. Maybe one of Eloise's rich distant relatives will knock off. She's into numerology and 2010's supposed to mean something.

"You write grants, right?"

"Ulysses S. Grantwriter," I said.

"You should help us get a grant."

"It doesn't work that way."

"You got yourself one."

"That's different," I said. "It's from the NEA. I'm an artist."

He complains he's poor, but he owns the house outright and the taxes on it are nothing. Last week I walked in on Mel and Eloise in their parlor entertaining who I presumed was a religious proselytizer – but it was a salesman pitching reverse mortgages to older couples.

"You're fifty-nine," I said. "Those are for people seventy-something."

"You're twenty-seven," he said. "How much are you in hock for school?"

I counted on my fingers. "Six figures."

"This guy here says I could get $70,000 for the property, square away. And we still get to live here."

Cash flow dilemma. I would have suggested investing in a hydroponic, but on Sundays the Slopers are big-box Christian people, so that's off the table.

"I can't listen to you get swindled, Mel."

"We could do a lot on seventy-grand."

"You can do a lot less than you think."

Eloise is the woman at whom menopausal commercials are aimed. Her lunch is a can of sparkling wine and nachos encased in cold cheese. Pedialyte is her hangover antidote. QVC is her kryptonite.

"What kind of books do you read, Eloise?" I was just making small talk.

"Oh, Christian books," she said. "You know, God."

"And Mel, what does he read?"

"Oh, books on NASCAR."

The $400-a-month rental arrangement includes meals. It doesn't matter for how much the room rented for, Eloise would rather it was occupied than vacant. She's careful around my exposures, she looks at them but not into them, and I can't blame her because I don't see that deeply into them myself. But she does like my Marlene Dietrich. And she wonders why I won't photograph her.

"They're daguerreotypes. Mel helped me build the camera. You know, orotones. Old-timey pictures with long exposures," I explained.

"I have plenty of time," Eloise said. "Nothing but."

If she's not in front of the television she's on the phone with her friends at the nursery. Her peonies are blooming late: it's the *crisis du jour*. The Slopers' rotary phone pegged to the wall recalls the times I had to call home from parochial school for fighting on the playground, or skipping out on Mass.

I told her, "You can upgrade telephones. Get a cordless, or a mobile. That way you could just chat away in the garden."

Eloise looked at me funny. She had unsightly skin tags on her neck. "What, and be that crazy lady who talks to her plants?" When she laughed it was double-EE tumultuous inside her shirt. "Besides, who would ever call me?"

She had a very good point.

Mel was drafted in 1969. He listened to it on the radio. His lottery number was 4. This, apparently, is why he doesn't celebrate his birthday. He spent the final years of the Vietnam War in the motor pool at Fort Ord until he couldn't take it any longer, polishing Jeeps, fellating brass, that he moved out of the barracks and shacked up with a chemist at U.C.L.A. and, every week before his psychiatric exam, got loaded on different analgesics, Quaaludes, laboratory-pure cocaine, to approximate schizophrenia. It all sounded very Warhol-ian, his honorable discharge.

He was excited to show off his latest project. I expected him to unveil a Bel-Air or a golden Datzun 240Z, something with wings and get-up, a muscle car, but not this: an amalgam of parts, colors and fuselage, sidings of an Escalade, undercarriage of a Volt, breathtaking in its audacity, the sort of vehicle a lesser man would string together using duct tape and bailing wire. In the factory Mel was no grease monkey. He attached fenders. The noise never did bother him, so he eschewed the ear plugs and safety gear. From a practical standpoint, absconding with these parts was a logistical impossibility: but all of his cohort were complicit: the security details, inventory control: a factory culture that turned to sabotage once everyone felt the steady erosion of their benefits and the inevitability of the pink slips.

I asked, "Eloise doesn't know about this?"

"She doesn't know. She does whatever it is childless women do. I don't bother with any of that. She lets me alone, and I let her alone … in love with her doctors on the soaps."

In June her moods were no better than Mel's. Eavesdropping on their Ralph-and-Alice Kramden kitchen banter one day I overheard Mel, late afternoon, posturing for food.

"I'm hungry," he told Eloise. "What's there for me to eat?"

She went bezerk in the pantry. "Meat! Meat! Meat! Meat! What else is there in this house! When is there ever anything else! Dairy. Cheese. Butter. Meat! It's all we ever have."

It was a good marriage. Mel limited his indiscretions to the local bars; he never willingly slept on the couch. He was maudlin when her mood was low. I suggested that he outfit himself in a good suit and take her dancing and out to a nice dinner.

"That's the ticket," he said. "Like an Applebee's."

Mel likes to play the bumpkin, but in his youth, Eloise tells me, he was arrestingly bright and handsome. "When I was your age, the future looked cheerful," he said. "We weren't going to be broke at fifty-nine, and jobless." He worked on the calluses on his palms with a pumice stone.

"You built this," I said, beholding his latest flame. "What's it named?"

"Meloise," he said, licking the grease on his thumb.

Clever.

"I've never taken her out before," he said, twirling the keys like vice cops do handcuffs.

Maiden voyage. Near the Wayne State campus Mel Sloper says the recession's over and that he's going to spend in defiance of the bad economy. In Royal Oak he's cursing the Mexicans taking our jobs.

He was born in Sheboygan. I didn't know where that was. He held up his left hand, as all left hands are shaped like Michigan. Sheboygan was the callous beneath his ring finger.

"Canada's right there," I said, pointing up to nothing.

Detroit. It was, as the song goes, so cold in the D. Mel gave me the grand tour. We cruised past the sulking hulks, the reverb of American industrial misfortune: The Fort Shelby Hotel, The Statler, Joe Muer's. A time so severely at ebb that rescue seemed inconceivable.

Meloise's front seats are leather and her rear seats are cloth. The engine didn't purr. When I rolled down my window, the trunk popped open.

With this kind of ingenuity, I know we can beat the Chinese.

As he drove her Mel pointed and narrated. The freeways were empty; half of Michigan had bailed. Once I got the window down I ingested the sky, hair trailing and whipping around, Medusa-like. When he tired of talking Mel put a Red Foxx cassette in the tape deck, pealing with unemployable idiot laughter. I'm not sure what's funny, but I go along with it. It feels good to laugh, really truly. Everything's on its head, topsy turvy. We never had it so good.

Evidence that gift-giving is Mel's love language with his niece: he paid seventeen dollars for a Sequoia germination kit – a pine cone in a fancy aluminum can. And he never once talked poorly of her mother.

In Pontiac we barrel over railroad tracks. Soaring. On the concrete sidings of the railroad spurs is written: *I am Legit* and other, less discernable graffiti. As we land Mel is thrown forward, telling me, "I don't care who your celebrity crush is, just so long as it's not my sister."

Becca was a minor big deal a few decades ago, until she bankrupted her record label. Too much was made of her one hit. Real fame in those days was the Dick Cavett program, but she only managed a cameo on Wally George's Hot Seat. Her cache petered out and she hit the booze and Mel had nothing more to say.

"Becca cut this album in a day," he said, fishing through one of the boxes in the backseat, his left wrist guiding Meloise, two cans of beer sloshing in the console. "If I can find it. Ah, here. *One* day. I was at the sessions and most of her concerts. When she sang, the ladies swooned. The *ladies*," he said. "Imagine that."

They look related. I saw the resemblance in their jawlines. Becca Carmichael, *nee* Sloper, draped in sequins, her hair Gericurled – album covers in the days before Photoshop, when if you were a promoter you drove a stone pleasure boat like Meloise and if your talent wasn't a 10 you used a soft lens for her headshots.

"I was at one of her venues," Mel said, "it was all poorly wired up top, slipshod work, and with everyone smoking and the dry ice, the smoke detectors went off. When the cops rushed in, she started taunting them. And then she sort-of lost interest in singing for the night, climbed down into the front row, and laid in my lap and cried."

"Your lap?"

"Right here," Mel said, patting his groin.

Raleigh's was Detroit's musical consignment. Waifish teens congregated out front, boys with big hair and mascara, guitars strapped to shoulders. Grunge chic. They looked convincingly homeless. I helped Sloper in with his boxes, except for his sister's album, which I thought should stay in the family.

Paper is heavy. Vinyl is heavy. We slogged it inside. "I've never done this before," Mel told the buy-back clerk. "Times are hard."

Sloper leaned on the counter as the clerk sifted through and counted. I learned a lot about Mel from his music. He had gone through a Herb Alpert phase in the 70s, whipped cream and all, and a Black Flag one in the 80s. He owned the *Footloose* soundtrack and the greatest ticklings of Liberace.

"Ten dollars, guys."

"Ten bucks," Sloper repeated. "I must have paid a thousand for these. They must be worth something."

"Ten in cash, or twenty in trade."

"Trade?"

"It's a twenty dollar coupon," the clerk explained, writing it out on a pink slip which he stamped and signed.

"This here is Emmylou Harris," Mel said, holding hers' up, nonplussed.

"Don't get down," I told Mel. "Good time to buy, bad time to sell."

Mel shook his head, unbelieving, and held the slip like the skeptics taking the Eucharist – saltine crackers transmogrified into the body of Christ – in the stadiums where he worships Sundays and which I watch on television. I can see it in their faces. They don't dispute there's a Lord. They just can't find Him. Without football their Sabbath is ruined.

Mel's still pissed. He claims the good people of Detroit are throwing out their commemorative Inauguration papers. His friends who dumpster dive told him so. Mel would get hired somewhere, as a mechanic, a machinist. Of course, he's going about it all wrong. You don't put on your Sunday clothes and beat the pavement chatting it up in corporate lobbies with dunce secretaries for vacancies they don't know about or, if they did, would reveal only to their friends. These days it's all computerized. This frustrates Mel, confuses him. He would rather gladhand and cajole. He's old school that way.

Eloise is getting fatter, succored by prosecco. Avon's a fine gig, but she's thinking of switching to Mary Kay. She wants that pink Cadillac.

The Slopers are not the Huxstables and Mel is not the Fonz. All his savings were sunk in tanking stocks. For decades he trusted his institutionalized intuition, the designs of the brokers and the senators. Today gold is up, platinum is down, but what little he's got, he's got in silver. Eloise doesn't know about it. Things are bad, getting worse, but never mind that. Back to his garage goes Mel. The garage, his Maginot Line.

Or Current Resident

The minute Karina landed at SFO – an hour late from Kennedy, into a headwind – Andres called to tell her to hurry over. Their POD had arrived, but the permits to keep it legally parked on Hayes Street were missing.

It took her 30 minutes to drive to Alamo Square, circling the block three times before finding an open spot to park, on Steiner, directly across from the Painted Ladies, from that TV show she loved growing up, *Full House*, with those darling twins.

"You always were great at parallel parking," Andres said.

Karina was from originally from Redondo Beach, in Southern California. Practically born in a car, with hair thick as an afghan hound's, she surrounded herself with plastic figurines in high school, friends who looked as if they were carved from a mold in a factory. If you got too close you could see the makeup she insisted she needed at all times, even on the weekends, when she rarely left the house.

"How was your flight?"

"Fine. I was in in the fast lane and got honked at going 85."

"Home sweet home," he said.

In a life on the road it was generally safer to accelerate than to brake. Their new West Coast apartment, despite the freshly painted smell – Navajo white, two coats – was as fragrant as fried sage with a dynamite view of the Golden Gate

Bridge, for which she was sure they were paying extra: $2,800, non-rent controlled. (*When did that stop being a lot of money?* she asked her parents, rhetorically.) It had been previously sub-let to a pastry chef with a small, domesticated pig, a cute, kid-friendly apartment with an elevator and no doorman to tip at the end of the year. She moved back to California excited again for earthquakes and looking forward to fresh cuisine, green salads, her health. When word of Andres' transfer from the Miami Financial Center came through, he asked Karina point-blank, "If you could live anywhere, where would it be?", and she said LA, of course, then San Francisco, in that order. Los Angeles was clean and magical and the ceviche was fresh and the horchata cold. She had never lived north, longitudinally, of the Hollywood sign.

"I have a surprise for you," Andres said, tossing her the key to the POD. "Open it."

It was a 17' shipping container, the two-bedroom model. Karina unlocked the deadbolt and lifted the sliding accordion door.

"You've got to be kidding me," she said.

There had been some mix-up. It wasn't their furniture.

There was no playbook for moving across the country. Moving was a trauma. She was tired of living out of a suitcase, in hotels and on friends' couches, indebted to family and acquaintances she didn't talk to often or even like that much. But it was worth it. Miami had been a suicide to their conjugal happiness. Andres had been acting more gangrenous toward her in recent years, as if he was suddenly re-born, except in an ice bath. She knew California would be good for him – no more Cuban heiresses changing their surnames, downplaying their wealth. No more Human Tetris commutes downtown.

"At least the key works," he said.

How could he be so dense? Where did it go? Her creaky rocking chair. Her wardrobe the size of the garment district. The wedding ring that belonged to her grandmother. All of their wedding presents. Her dowry. It was part of her family.

"You need to take care of this. Call the company and yell at someone."

"Just as a short term solution ..." Andres said, crawling inside the unit, uncovering boxes, inspecting shelves, "... let's unpack the bed."

"I am *not* sleeping in another hotel."

"Just the bed," he repeated.

"How are we going to explain that when they finally show up?"

"If they show up, we'll say we hired some help to unload the POD."

"And then?"

"And then we'll just blame the imaginary help."

A spouse is supposed to carry his weight, hold the heavier side sometimes, as with the big honking armoire they worked to maneuver into the elevator lined with blue padding. Karina panicked quietly and rhetorically to herself (*What if it was delivered to the right address, and what if we're neighbors, and if so can we just swap apartments? What if they're judging us for our cheap dishware?*). Nothing was labeled. This other couple had better taste, a better sense of humor; their art was smarter, the pewter more refined. Their cookware were in sets, not in hodgepodge. No board games, not even a deck of cards. A stealthier blender. And the cowboy boots he found fit Andres, a pretend cowboy, size 10EE, as if he had been outfitted by a complete stranger. To Karina all of this was like inheriting a new life, as if they had been given new identities, the old ones wiped out, the slate clean.

"Found their passports!" Andres exclaimed.

And birth certificates. Emily Warren (DOB: 07/14/85) had most recently travelled to Belize; her passport photo looked as if it had been taken in one of those glamour shot studios in Sears. Vivek Singh, fiercely bearded and smartly dressed and twenty-seven days younger than Emily, had just had his passport renewed. On their birth certificates, her eyes were blue; he weighed 5 lbs 4ozs and was delivered in Ann Arbor, MI, by one Dr. Boone Breech – two months premature, Karina guessed. She couldn't even remember what hospital she was born in, but now she knew theirs, and Vivek's gargle stains on his shaving mirror, and (the *coup de grace*), a record player, which she had never owned and which fascinated her, the way the arm slid across and knew when to lift itself up and deposit the needle back at the beginning, with boxes and boxes of heavy, exotic, old vinyl. Dust was the enemy of fidelity. It put Karina's old compact disc collection to shame.

There was a lot to be done, every day, and even on Sundays Andres was a constant paragon of busyness. It was a revolt against his early life, all those anarchies, all that poorly channeled, waylaid angst. Absentmindedly, for months before their move across the country, he had been taking the wrong vitamin most mornings – her pre-natal vitamins – in a hurry to get out the door and *ahead*. Truth be told, Karina wanted to be a wife, not a mother. Marriage had been on the tippy-top of her list of things to do before she turned 30. At a shotgun wedding, someone has to pull the trigger; she had want-ed to elope so badly, a small obscure ceremony, but her family talk-ed her out of it because they wanted to pay for a big wedding and it would hurt Karina's pastor's feelings if she didn't let him officiate. She found it hard after the happy ending – the walking down the aisle – was over. After a day of wedded bliss they hadn't intertwined so much as they were orbiting one another's lives by happenstance. Like any sport, a relationship was a question of possession, and for all of his transgressions and turpitudes she forgave him and apol-ogized for him, like a benevolent tyrant canonizing a malevolent saint. Except for a co-ed dormitory at a summer camp when she was 17 she had never lived with other men, she had only lived among or encountered them, as one does in a movie theatre or an elevator.

Andres didn't bring much to the marriage as far as belongings or things went. Karina promised she wasn't the clingy type, but after two days she felt like saran wrap to him, and at Catalina Island on their honeymoon when he bought her cotton candy, a gossamer fantasy, she wondered who in her bridal party she would still be speaking to in 20 years – and two years later she knew the answer. She was very thin then and very blonde and blushing immodestly from all Andres' flattery and attention and at times she could still feel the paper cuts on her tongue from licking so many 'thank you' notes. In the evenings they burned marshmallows black and read to one another from the same story collection. He told her about his Senior Prom, at Richard Nixon's Presidential Library, when he snuck away to dance with his date on Dick and Pat's grave (with Checkers, their beloved dog, buried between). Of the hundred guests they had invited to the wedding, two were packing: one had a pistol in his fanny pack and another, Andres' Uncle Kurt, a derringer in a boot, just in case anyone objected.

Karina's daytime mind was a careless aviary. She thought she had put all of these memories away, sequestered them somewhere. She was sometimes nostalgic for the bad times ... that is, once she found she could survive difficult episodes – knock-down, drag-out fights, until they were on the very cusp of divorce – that turned out to be okay in the end, a simple disagreement, just one of those happy tragedies of false consequence. She found more faults with Andres as the years went on, and he was more honest about them, and all she could do was enjoy him and the fact of them, together, though she could not even tell the story of it, as if her past had been infiltrated or fabricated, or both. They did not take as many photos together as she'd have liked – at least, not as many as Emily and Vivek had.

"Now look at this couple," Andres said, after finding one of their wedding albums. "Here are two people where no one's saying, 'I'm going to break that marriage up.'"

"The furniture says it," Karina said.

That night, to celebrate and de-stress, they went out to take San Francisco not so much by storm or monsoon, but by light drizzle. They were getting too old to be out late blathering and sloshing together, arm in arm, song after song. Two drinks was her limit. They found a tony-looking bar in Hayes Valley, near City Hall. Karina took short, steady sips.

"Little pink cocktails for you and me," Andres said, toasting her.

His career in the financial sector helped him in his marriage. He had told Karina that being around so many high-net-worth individuals taught him the humility and devotion he thought she needed.

"Forgive me for yawning," he said. "Big day tomorrow."

He appeared cavalier, or worse, apathetic when he was on deadline, when in fact he was a cauldron inside.

"You'll do great."

"I need a secretary," he said.

"First you need to learn to write legibly. Then you can get a secretary."

What he needed at night was a few too many. Around them and stacked up three-deep at the bar were buttoned up people, people in rough shape, sordid people, talkers, listeners, all walks, a mongrel compost of humanity. Karina was all turned around. The days were a blur, a mesh of rules … wear your helmet, eat your Wheaties. Some years you want a complete do-over. Last year it was 'make money' and this year it was 'make babies.' Cocktails were incongruent with her fitness goals. Andres had consumed his first drink one slow and the second one way too fast, and was talking about all the things he promised her – a sumptuous, ornate kimono on their fifth wedding anniversary, for instance – when it wasn't about things at all, and why wouldn't he put his finger on it: she doesn't want his kids or anyone's, she wants to find and dabble in the unknown, and the difference between them was, her unknown is people and his unknown, Andres, is nature, security, fatherhood. It wasn't things and it wasn't even joy that Karina wanted, but pleasure, bottomless, ceaseless pleasure. But it didn't look to her like he recognized any of this in her face: martinis tend to reduce all men to the obvious.

After a week in Alamo Square Karina had not settled in, while Andres was finding his legs at work, twelve hours a day, loitering late at the office, noosing himself up before meetings with a Double Windsor knot, wearing inconspicuous wingtips. Marathon days. Financial news was, to Karina, boring as ballet, but it was all he could talk about when he entered the door and she asked 'How was your day?' and he never answered something along the lines of 'My salad at the downstairs cafe usually comes with three cherry tomatoes, but today it came with five!' but instead with:

"Caught you napping."

"I was not. I just closed my eyes."

"You were snoring."

"I don't snore. I've never heard myself snore. Girls don't snore."

"Got a small raise today."

"Great," she said. "What are we spending it on?"

"Our landlord will probably spend it," he said.

Raises should come in lump sums. Andres resented how power was stratified: they'll drug test lower-level associates such as himself, but they won't test a CEO, for example, who commanded a large salary and jettisoned all responsibility. In response, he tried not to use or be seen with any Styrofoam at work, aware of how terrible it was for the environment and that he himself would decompose at least a century before those egg-white and spongy coffee cups did.

"Oh, and something else funny happened today," Andres said.

It felt like a gunshot, he said, when he felt something hit his shoulder near the Flood Building on Market Street. He patted his arm, expecting blood, but his shirt was wet and clear. A bird had shat on him from the 17th floor. From that altitude it felt like a dime or a bullet had dropped on him.

Karina laughed at this, which made her aware of how little she had laughed recently. She ought to have kissed Andres, or thanked him. He was making this life happen. He was striving. He kept trying even if it was to no avail. Trying mattered, sometimes even more than succeeding. Effort. His monochromatic wardrobe. The few colors. Thirty-one years old was too late for anything but the commencement of his long delayed manhood. He took joy in his work. He was not, like her, a square peg moving into a round hole. It was the urban combat he was prepared for, carrying himself like a prince, albeit a deposed one. He spent three fifteen minute breaks and one pack of Lucky Strikes trying to perfect the Paul-Henried-*Now-Voyager*-two-cigarettes-at-a-time thing, to impress his co-workers. Beating others' personal bests. They had come all this way. The workhorses of the department. Asked to surrender his Fridays and he assented. *Yes sir, happy to.* It's not a career, it's a casino, and he still doesn't know how to balance three accounts, then three becomes five. The art of hustling. Sometimes he forgets to breathe.

Seven p.m. on a Tuesday night and Karina still had not dressed, while Andres had time to go to the grocery store and find a whole ripe pineapple and some baby's breath to put into one of Emily's vases, a Faberge, cracked just right and dinged. Some days you just can't get out of bed,

Karina wanted to say. Sleeping a life away isn't a bad way to live, there are worse ways. The bed is safe. There's no harm in bed. She could lay there forever in the lovely horizontalism and be perfectly safe, this darling girl, downright deadly with her darlingness. It was around the time of year – February 29th, which comes once every four years – when people either quit or forget their New Year's resolutions, as she had neglected hers.

"I don't know what to tell you," she said. "I've been suddenly very tired lately. I don't have any answers. I don't even have any questions. It's called nesting, I guess."

Her childhood was an intractably splendid infinity of strangeness. California – she called it her *California 2.0* – was extra daylight, a new religion ... but still, no children was her policy – she didn't tell Andres her reasons – because she was afraid she wouldn't be able to lose the weight, and because they, children, smile too much.

"If we have a daughter," he said, patting her stomach as if conception was indeed immaculate, "I don't know what to name her."

"We could name her Anne."

"And her middle name?"

"I don't know. Boleyn?"

Epiphanies simmer and Karina only noticed them once they boiled. So far away here. Beyond exile. Huddling up with coffee. Cardigan weather. For a week she had been driving around with a parking ticket affixed to her rental car's windshield. A child or a good job doesn't make one an adult. The thought of playdates terrified her. It's not the kids she feared but their parents. Because labors of love are still labors. In Los Angeles – not like here, with Alcatraz and sharks – you could swim far enough out to where you're not sure if you have the strength to swim back. They rusted out, the hoses connected to outdoor pipes, as a child; she drank rust. When her pierced ears closed up in the 4th grade her friends heated up a sewing needle with a Bic lighter and re-pierced them – she still had the scar, and often felt it for proof that she actually had a past.

"You look off today," Andres said.

"I feel off."

"Happy Leap Day," he said.

"It's not a real day," she said. "Today is supposed to be March already."

"I think you're amazing," he said.

"But why?"

"What do you mean 'why'?"

"Sometimes a woman needs to hear why."

She wanted to shoot him, for no reason, one of the many menacing looks in her arsenal. She had a robust vocabulary of expressions, whereas he won by words and patience, by consolation and flattery and not getting into scrums, known for his ability to out-sit everyone, corporate endurance, extending meetings until he got everything he wants, controlling the minutes. He tried to reassure her that San Francisco was a city for women, where females dominated, but if that was true then why was her resentment so new, so strong? Her wedding ring never used to budge, and lately she had begun to twist it, a nervous habit at first. She had also cut herself cleaning the blades of the garbage disposal, her hand swallowed by the gaping drain. Scary, but no stitches. It felt that she was finding her way through life as if crawling through a buttonhole. Andres had given her love, yes, and an attractive shock of gray hair and a bouquet of hydrangeas that dried out beautifully and were as forever as the diamonds on her wedding ring. What he lacked in *savoir faire* he made up for as an A-1, top-flite fabulously coiffed and studded-out breadwinner. There had been no first dance at their wedding, just some passed *hors doerves* by the catering staff. Their vacation plans never seemed to materialize after their honeymoon, and they were practically bankrupted because of their friends' far flung destination weddings, where Andres was usually asked to be a groomsman at the last minute so that there were as many boys as girls in the wedding party. Symmetry mattered.

Emily and Vivek never did come for their things. It was as if they didn't exist, or had died, or were playing a protracted practical joke. After a month of enjoying her new garments – they fit her nicely, as if Emily was an older sister – Karina donated them all to a charity that clothed women exiting prison.

She had been learning San Francisco, on foot, from the Marina to the Bayview, but especially the TL, as it was called by the locals, and Nob Hill, fascinated by the slang she overheard on streetcars, mixed in with the cat-calls – she would pause and excuse herself and ask what it all meant and if it was okay if she, a white girl from the suburbs, could also use it without sounding silly or insensitive. She saw all kinds of life, and wanted to get closer to it, because there's scum you can see a mile away (Andres' office was on the 58th floor of the Transamerica Building, she could see him sometimes through her binoculars) and then there's the scum you can only see up close. Her leisure was the most important thing. She didn't want to live like everyone else, restraining herself, keeping her hopes so miniscule like the moms she saw – in the stroller-patrol that was Divisadero St. in the daytime – because children are cruel in places where naptime is strictly enforced.

Irregular exercise was best. One afternoon outside of Finnegan's Wake near Kezar Stadium she was feeling flirty and let three men – the ruins of people who used to be in their right minds – buy her kamikazes, doubles, in exchange for her life story.

"As long as I don't have to start at the beginning," she said.

On the TV above, Andrew Cashner, hurling against the Giants, was down 4 runs in the 2nd inning and pressing.

"Can you turn the channel?" she asked the bartender.

"To what?"

"Hm," she said. "Home Shopping Network?"

She lived like she was retired, she told the guys, happy laborers swilling Newcastles, but it hadn't always been the case: she was actually very well-traveled, the trouble was (and it didn't matter if they believed her or not) that her travels to Europe and France and French films didn't make her want to smoke, or speak three languages, or be French. What mattered was poking her husband in the side so she'd get a picture of him smiling walking back up the aisle. This picture of her with a husband, not a father

— this man of hers who, when office-mates showed off pictures and sometimes ultrasound screenshots of their kids and kids-to-be, didn't recoil, or shudder, just smiled and said *Awwwwwww*.

"He doesn't know," Karina said, "that I've been sabotaging my birth control. Or trying to, at least."

"Poking holes in his rubbers?" the bartender asked.

"Even better," she said. "I never went off of the pill."

"I have a son," the bartender said. "Could have just as well been a girl." He wiped the wood in front of Karina with a soiled towel in short, bitter, concentric circles.

"It's all a matter of rolling the chromosomic dice," she said.

"This bitch is crazy," she overheard.

"I have my reasons," she shot back.

Someone said, "I hope you find whatever you're looking for, miss."

"I wasn't looking for anything," she said, to no-one, every-one. "Don't patronize me."

Karina had always been cold and calculating in revenge, to this man, all men, Andres especially. After all, *he* was the one impregnating *her*.

We Don't Talk About It

Dog days, indeed. Terrible, painful drought. It hadn't rained in so long that the residents of Devore — and all across Southern California — had stopped carrying umbrellas in cloudy weather, even when the forecast called for rain, as if they didn't believe it would ever rain again.

Marco Wedding's Oldsmobile sat fallow in his driveway, caked in dirt. His girls, Carly and Robin, were 9 and 7; their favorite vegetable candy corn. On the weekends the four of them went bowling as a family at Memories Lanes. Pete Wilson was governor.

The house of his dreams, which he had a 30-year mortgage on, had been built in 1929 on a two-acre lot in the foothills, overlooking the I-15 freeway that snaked through the Cajon Pass toward Las Vegas, and points east. It was rumored that in the early '30s William Randolph Hearst stashed several of his mistresses in the upstairs quarters to keep them out of sight, and that Al Capone would sometimes lodge in the in-law unit above the garage as a guest before the long drive to Two Bunch Palms, his desert hideaway. In the permits and paperwork that came with the house Marco learned this and more: how the workers who built it had unearthed arrowheads from the Morongo Indian tribe and a pair of femurs presumed to be human, but which actually belonged to a horse.

Marco named the property 'Oleander.' It was his Hermitage, his Versailles. He had loved the estate since he was eight years old, pedaling by it on the way to and from parochial school. He knew which flowers in the vast yard were edible and which, like the oleanders, he should avoid. The hedges, the grandeur – it took almost a century for cypresses to grow that stately and tall. A thicket of moss flourished on one side of the roof, the southerly facing side with all of the shade, and this to him – along with the ivy crawling up the wall – was the very personification of wealth: what his parents used to refer to as 'a ringer' or 'the real deal.' When he was a young man, Marco knew it would take a disconcerting fate or an insurance windfall from a premature death in his family for him to ever be able to afford it. In 1976, with his parents flying back from Greece after celebrating their 17th year of marriage, fate obliged. Their plane was never found, and PanAm owed Marco just enough (settlement-wise) for a down payment.

But even dead grass needs mowing. The drought changed the entire palette of Oleander. The grass in the front yard had caramelized, the dandelions were yellow, and a blight had begun to overwhelm the rosemary. Marco had just a few years before installed a complex RainBird system to keep the yard lush: what a waste now. He should have spent it on a succulent or an herb garden, which became more fragrant the less water they received, and were durable and hard to kill in any weather. The small orange grove in the backyard, too, was more fragrant without water, but the fruit suffered, the pulp bitter, and he could no longer juice them to enjoy with breakfast.

Over the years Oleander had been surrounded, besieged really, on all sides by a tract of modularized suburban homes, filled with families the Weddings waved to from the street and (with a certain exception) rarely associated with. Marco did not want himself or his family to live like other people. Getting excited about the local little league. Get excited about the new pastor at church. Things had changed radically since 1929 as the old neighborhood became less exclusive and more working class, and their wide beautiful street, Mayfield Avenue, was increasingly used as a bypass from Mount

Vernon Road and its dozens of unsynchronized stoplights. His wife, Garnet, had petitioned Devore's City Council to remedy this by installing three speed bumps – "for my children, and yours," she stated during public comment – and her persistence compelled the local police to station an empty cop car two houses over to slow motorists down to the posted limit of 25 mph. This dummy car was never moved or attended to, as if the cops had forgotten about it – its tires nearly flat, one of the windshield wipers was missing – such that Marco paid his girls $1 each every Sunday after their family bowling outing to hose it down (with a wax, he insisted) as he and Garnet sat on the porch in their deep Adirondacks with a can of cold beer, and Abernathy, the family Bernese, laying between them.

"The girls look the same," Garnet said.

Marco inspected Abernathy's collar. The phone number on his tag was no longer correct.

"It's not my fault they look the same," he said.

"It's half your fault," she said.

Garnet still had the lithe, tall figure of the champion figure skater she had been at 19, when she won a silver medal at the 1980 Olympics in Lake Placid. Refinement seemed to emanate from her, a bottomless fountain of chic. She was very much on demand as an ice dance instructor in Arrowhead Springs, just up the mountain. It was the kind of job she could do for life. Every morning she fed Abernathy two bagels, with lox, which he loved. He was the family mascot.

"It might get to 100 degrees tomorrow," she said, harpooning Abernathy's fur with her long fingers. "I told you this is too much dog."

"Scares off burglars," Marco said.

"Sure, he'll lick an intruder to death."

This sky. Marco recognized this sky. What made the sky blue, he reflected, was not space or the glare of the ocean, but the blues of mankind.

"Dad, I'm hungry," Carly yelled, running up the lawn, a filthy rag draped over her shoulder. Robin squeezed sponges out in the plastic bucket, making a face. She had scrubbed so hard, Marco thought she might rub off the police decals.

"It's about dinner time," Marco said. "What should we make tonight?"

"I dunno," the girls said, almost in unison.

They seemed to have no opinions or preferences, for anything. Marco's nicknames for them were Don't Know and Don't Care.

"Go get Grandma's recipes," Garnet said.

Carly ran inside to fetch the book of index cards, and as a family unit the Weddings leafed through them, careful not to smudge the fading pencillations.

"Chicken Piccata. We haven't had this one in a while," Robin said.

Marco held the card away from his eyes, which were going bad.

"One of the ingredients says 'pillow talk'," he said.

"That's paprika," Garnet said, without looking.

They prepared meals together, as a family. Marco marveled at how well their housekeeper ran the household. They never seemed to run out of ingredients. Everything was fresh, as if it had just been picked minutes before.

"Never trust an onion that doesn't make you cry," he said, wiping his eyes at the cutting board.

"Please don't use your jeans as a napkin," he told the girls as they sat down.

"Seconds?" he asked, once they cleared their plates.

But no, they were satisfied. Lately they ate like birds. Not malnourished, just slender. After dinner was cleared away and their bedtime came, he caught them rambunctious in the bedroom they shared, suffocated by rainbow wallpaper and magazine cut-outs of teen idols.

"What are you two doing? It's almost bedtime."

"I'm practicing driving a flying car," Robin said.

She was his favorite. Getting straight A's without studying. Winning without really trying.

"Where to?"

"The museum."

"You need history before you can have a museum."

"No, this is a museum of the future," Robin said. "Nothing's been invented yet."

They had all slept in the same bed as a family, the four of them, until Robin turned 3 and Carly 5, and it was decided that Garnet and Marco deserved some time alone at night. Together they would bunch under the covers and watch sitcoms, even though Marco despised having a TV in the bedroom. It was because of the canned laughter, he told the girls when they laughed at bad or crude jokes, but they didn't understand that those weren't live people in the audience. The laughing was a machine, he'd say. Still, they didn't want to believe it.

They were darling and they were very much his, down to their features and mannerisms. He would pay any amount, mortgage his life for them. They were not just his daughters but lately his best friends, and when they would ask where Mom was (working, usually), or why she wouldn't answer them or play with them at night, Marco didn't say because it was a strange, sad, distant time for Garnet, who had begun to subtly close herself up around happiness, like California poppies did in the springtime when there was too much sunlight.

Two of Garnet's older students – promising skaters, maybe not future Olympians but talented enough to tour with Disney on Ice – had just been killed in a team bus wreck after practice. Garnet was trailing the bus in her Mercedes and was the first on the scene. A wreck is never tidy. The first thing she saw, clambering into the ravine the bus had plummeted down, was a severed limb.

It was the surfeit of death and hurt that seemed to cripple her. She immersed herself in teaching, food and sleep. To Marco it was as if she had consented to shaving off thin slices of her heart like a block of parmesan, until there was nothing left to grate, and he hoped for the girls' sake that her heart would grow back, soon, like a lizard's tail or the ivy enveloping the Spanish tiles overhead, clogging the gutters.

Or maybe she was much worse off than he had the courage to admit. Garnet had started to relinquish all of the parenting to him, and she refused nearly all invitations to be social with people he knew she loved. She had even withdrawn from her closest friends, the Coors', who were the only other (happily) married couple on Mayfield Avenue, in the house four doors down with the white Peugeot parked on the lawn. They shared a landscaper, just as their parents had shared bootleggers. On the 1-10 scale of family friendliness, Gary and Jean Coors were an 8. They made friendly bets on the Academy Awards. They were honest on their Census.

Migraines are the Best Excuse

Marco knew that once he and the girls left the Coors' house on Monday nights – another important ritual of cocktails, football and a barbeque – Jean would move the outdoor furniture inside so the sunlight wouldn't fade out the fabric. Mondays were Garnet's late nights at the training facility, and Jean liked to try out new dishes and recipes on guests. Garnet was among her best friends, and on occasion Jean would drive up in the middle of the week to watch her coach, even though the fluorescent glint off the ice hurt her eyes. A housewife is sensitive about her alone time in that she wants more of it, and Jean hired clairvoyants, tarot specialists, driving as far as Cucamonga and sometimes even to Santa Barbara for the cosmic edification that eluded her in Devore. Still, she admired the proselytizers who came by politely with the informative and uplifting religious literature, though she never invited them inside her home. There was nothing Jean liked so much she'd go door to door for.

"Autumn used to come slow. Now it just slams you," Jean told Marco, crouching down to hug Robin, who recoiled at any physical attention. "How are you, little one?"

"She doesn't like cursive," Marco answered for her. "Do you?"

"Well, now," Jean said.

"It's like the food on her plate," Marco added. "She doesn't like her letters touching. Where's Gary?"

"He's inside, looking for Scotch tape, because he accidentally tore up a $100 check that came today, thinking it was junk mail. But it was actual money! Isn't that a hoot!"

Marco was titillated by the quaintness of the Coors' quiet married life. The Coors' didn't just finish each other's sentences; they started them. They were that couple whom the decks are stacked for, blessed with fabulous skin and late family mortality.

"Gary's also a little upset because the cobbler lost his shoes," Jean said.

"Our cobbler? What was his explanation?"

"All he said was 'Oops!'"

Gnats fly in swarms, and bees, and gangs. Swordfish on the grill, sweating lightly. Tin foil packets of potatoes. A pyramid of coals. The four of them ate and joked and Gary didn't emerge, not once, and Garnet, who promised to come over once her headache subsided, didn't show either.

"You know I heard a rumor ..." Jean was trying her best to keep Carly and Robin entertained as she cleared the table of its plastic cutlery and paper plates ..." that many years ago this whole area used to be a zoo. But there was a fire. And they never found some of the animals."

"Have you looked next door?" Robin asked.

Hello or goodbye, Jean waved the same. "Tell Garnet to feel better," Jean said as they were on their way out. "I know she's in a damaged place."

"I will, and thank you."

"You know, I've often wondered how you do it. Two kids, big house, two careers."

Marco looked at the girls.

"How do we do it?" he asked them.

"Mom makes twice what Dad makes," Carly said, a tinge of pride in her voice.

"More than twice," Robin corrected.

Unsuspected Depths

On her morning drives up the mountain, Garnet indulged in her past. She didn't just touch her life; she put it on the wall; framed it, admired it. In 1978 she and Marco were merely pen-pals – he had written her a letter, not a fan letter so much as a *"Hello, I saw you skate in Memphis, you came in third, can you explain what the difference between a Salchow and a toe loop is?"* and she wrote back promptly because she swore to respond to all of her fan mail, and soon they were sending one another letters, almost daily, from photos of each other to trinkets to full confessions. Marco was the most attractive young man and she was then a most susceptible girl, and when he mailed her a key to his apartment in case she was ever in San Francisco and needed a place to crash, she surprised herself by immediately interrupting her training and jumping on the first plane west. His apartment was less romantic than she imagined it would be; the neighborhood was seedy and the city was not as beautiful to her as the Ohio she had just left. Garnet seemed to love his squalid place though, the allure of strangers and criminals on the stoop, trouble for trouble's sake.

She wanted gold so bad, so very bad. Her favorite part about the skating federation was the perks: her European souvenirs: bringing back smells that didn't exist in the U.S., such as exotic detergents and cigarettes. Marco pretended not to notice her slight stutter. She stayed at his place for a week and he was a perfect gentleman, never once made a pass. Something, though, had made her cruel and quarrelsome; she chastised him and his living quarters, and then her mood would oscillate around to something that was, approximately, love. On a picnic at Golden Gate Park she used a tube of sunscreen to draw hearts on Marco's bare back as he napped in the sun. His body was a theology, a psalm of pectorals. That week with him, she knew, was a debt she could never forgive because it was her time she gave him, not money. When she returned to Ohio he did not kiss her goodbye and they went back to writing letters but his handwriting worsened – slanted letters that began to look like a doctor's prescription, so slanted she was afraid they would topple over, right there off the page. For the entire calendar year of 1979 she stopped writing Marco, to focus on the Games.

Talent was the only pure thing.

Spare Me Your Ice Queen

Garnet's students ranged from 5 to 19, most of them from the kind of families who wore the same shirt at amusement parks and took pictures with the kids lined up tallest to shortest, bookended by Disney characters. It was not a time in their lives to count calories, which she had them do. She kept her own girls as far from the sport as possible.

"Hi, coach."

"Gracie," she acknowledged.

Somber mood, somber. The facility was hushed, in honor of its dead. In every corner – lining the foyer, Garnet's office, the locker rooms – there were happy flowers, sad flowers, roses for victory, roses in memorial wreaths. Their names were Florence Chen, Blake Ross. The year's successes would be dedicated to them. The bus driver, also, had died in the wreck.

"I did 500 pushups today."

"It's not true," another girl said. "She only did 470. I counted."

Vines of white beauty, carpeting the ice. Beds of lisianthus. Café au lait dahlias. Garnet vaguely remembered the weight of the silver bauble of minor hardware around her neck after she fell during the long program. Then, those flowers, a deluge of condolences and polite applause. It was the best thing that ever happened, and not just for her career. It gave her true humility. On the podium, she recalled, the weight was not heavy. Light as air.

"Today we work on your Lutz," she told Gracie.

The girl laced up and loped onto the ice. She was a shoo-in for Lillehammer and she knew it. Garnet cued up her music. It was her favorite part of skating: the choreography. Suddenly Gracie stopped.

"Something wrong?"

"I really hate this song," she said.

"It's Prokovief," Garnet said. "He's a winner."

"I can't hum to it."

A dream is something you work toward. A fantasy is something that will never happen. Gracie wanted virtually no body fat. She punished her body. Still, the fire inside her was not hot enough.

"What do you recommend?"

"Do you have any Mariah Carey?"

"The judges hate Baroque," Garnet said.

One of the benefits for most skating enthusiasts was an appreciation for classical music. Garnet was hard on Gracie because she needed to learn to handle it, because deep down she *could* handle it, but perhaps this was why all of the books she read on her way to competitions took place in outer space.

"Let's compromise," Garnet said, fishing through her cassettes, "with Lizst."

At 13 years old Gracie couldn't pick Lizst out of a lineup, but his wide leaps and terrifying octaves were going to make her a household name, maybe even get her on a Wheaties' box. It appalled Garnet how few of her students understood the high *dra-*

ma behind a skate: what you wanted in a song was obscurity and crescendo, harmonizing with the sizzle of a skate carving up ice.

Brahms was serviceable, in a pinch. Tchaikovsky was a dope.

I Didn't Just Love You

Marco didn't have to keep his job, but with the girls in school, he did. It was macabre, soulless work, and it occurred to him that he spent most days in places he didn't wish to be – work, home, his car. A while ago he started losing his hair. It could have been anything – stress, a new shampoo – but it wasn't. He was getting older. Age was the culprit.

Garnet called him at 4 p.m. on his car phone.

"How was work?"

"Fine," he said. "Meetings. Steering Committee."

"Any exciting decisions?"

"Yes, in fact." He switched to his left ear, merging onto the freeway. "They elected to lobotomize me, 5 votes to 2."

Garnet didn't laugh. Their housekeeper, Miranda, who came twice a week and sometimes helped with meals and babysitting, had had a strange afternoon, apparently. Her cake didn't rise as she wanted it to. She guessed she didn't beat her eggs enough. Perhaps an ingredient was missing.

"Why is she baking a cake?"

Then, Marco realized.

"Oh, no."

"You forgot."

Garnet kept a wine key in her purse for this very reason: spousal let-downs.

"Whose birthday is it?"

"The birthday of our marriage," Garnet said.

He couldn't believe he was one of those guys who would forget when he was married. He blamed it on the fact that it was nowhere on a calendar. The years had gotten away from him.

"Alright," Marco said. "Damage control. I love you. Congratulations and many happy returns, and don't hang up or chastise me, at least not too hard, not today, because we both know that somewhere in America, right now, the most romantic man in the world is going to the drugstore for a plush cupid, some Bon-Bons and a bottle of California champagne.

And that man is me."

That's the Story. I Lost. I Quit.

In those years when they first met Garnet seemed to be always moving, always in motion, like a cement truck. She was the kind of American abroad the emissaries at the embassy wished she wouldn't be. It was only after her Olympic disaster that she had time to calm herself, refocus, be anonymous. In 1981 Marco enrolled at the University of La Verne, near Pomona, the crossroads of three freeways, with virtually nothing and no-one.

Armed with this knowledge, Garnet decided she would enroll there too.

Self-reliance is not one lecture; it takes a few semesters. They rekindled their fledgling romance in the turbulence of Finals week, exams and cramming and too much caffeine. Marco was mourning the recent loss of his parents – the insurance money was no consolation, and neither was Garnet. She didn't know what to say or how to console him. Her *great*-grandparents were still alive, so what did she know of death? As she read more widely for her assignments she began to identify closest with Marco's least liked character in all of literature – Kathy, from John Steinbeck's *East of Eden*. Come exam time she had nerves of peanut brittle, despite her training and experience on the world's biggest stage. Crowds did not make her nervous. Blue Books did.

La Verne was hushed whispers, a Scaramouche of lipstick on cigarette butts and what-do-you-do-for-a-living, my-father-is-so-and-so. College had made her pale and sallow, like she had blown her own fire out, or was made-up each morning by a clown. The photos she put up in her dorm somehow made it feel less like home. Marco won her by attrition. He was always around. He carried her books. He was beginning to inhabit her, learning her skin, her imperfections and selfishnesses. He had dated a number of palindromes – a Hannah, a Nan – to where it became a running joke in his fraternity. Garnet knew that his brothers gave girls consecutive roman numerals: Hannah was Lady VI, Nan Lady VII, but what she didn't know was that she was Garnet, Lady I.

His first, and last.

I'm Not Sure How to Tell You

On date nights when they could afford it Marco would often quote Gene McCarthy – "*Never look at a woman reading a menu*" – and there came a point in their nights together where Garnet could undo everything – all of the mistakes and trespasses – and there was also a point where she could ruin the otherwise perfect evening.

"Am I a labor of love or lust?" she asked one night, over Italian food, the butter for the bread on the table not soft enough for her.

"Oh, dear," he said.

He wanted nothing from her. Everyone else wanted a piece, a photo, an autograph, and endorsements. And all she wanted – from before the Olympics – was a cherry red Ford Mustang. She pleaded and begged her grandparents for it. As a gift, a hard-earned reward. And when she got and promptly totaled the Mustang, wrapping it around a telephone pole – they had tied a big white bow on it and even filled the gas tank – she didn't visit them for two years, leaving them to think she was spoiled and ungrateful from her time in the limelight.

Marco seemed to enjoy this ballistic element to her storytelling. He was a George Washington-cherry-tree, Davy-Crockett-kilt-him-a-bear-when-he-was-only-three kind of listener. If she had told him she actually won gold he'd have believed her, though he watched her on the television and emitted an animal-like pain when she fell. He believed her because he wanted to.

"See that man over there?" she said.

A few tables over, a man dined alone, smiling shyly, sneaking furtive glances.

"Who's that?"

"A shy fan."

"You mean, he stalks you?"

"Haven't you noticed? Besides, he's harmless."

"I'm going to say something to him."

"No, don't," she said. "I kind of like it. He looks after me."

Marco offered to pour her another glass of moscato, but Garnet shook her head no.

"I wonder what our kids would look like," she said.

Marco opened his wallet, removing a faded, folded picture.

"Here," he said.

"This is you?"

"Ugly babies become pretty people."

"Some do. I can't believe you carry a picture of yourself in your wallet."

"That's not me. I was seven. That's my brother."

He looked nothing like his brother's baby photos, but who does? Children were all she could think about suddenly. Either Marco wasn't taking her hints or paying any attention to Garnet's waistline. She kept growing and she began to swell and knew she had to break the news to him and didn't want to do so gently. The only person she trusted was her first skating instructor who did not assure her that her career *wasn't* over, but who told her that no matter how much money you have, it's never enough: you'll always be broke when you decide to have kids.

The Most Enormous No

To celebrate her college graduation — she was still not showing, three months along with Carly — Garnet's parents threw her a block party in Columbus and invited the media but not Marco, when her father said she was:

"Too young for a wedding, especially this one."

The Beatles were on loud – the whole neighborhood had turned out just to see her.

"You taught me how to drive to this album," Garnet said.

"Don't think I forgot it for one minute," he said, and opened the garage door with his new clicker, unveiling a sporty orange Plymouth Roadrunner with a four-track cassette player.

"Your chariot awaits," he said.

She looked under the hood. It was only a four-cylinder. After all she had been through.

"Is this for graduating or medaling?" she asked.

"You look disappointed," her father said.

Block parties were his signature way of showing off. His attitude was one of flying-the-American-flag-in-the-yard-until-it's-tattered, a patriotism that repelled Garnet every canned food drive and Flag Day.

"I guess I was hoping for a vacation," she said.

"Where to?"

Garnet had traveled everywhere, but had gone nowhere. She knew airports and airport hotels and airport food.

"Aruba."

"But you hate flying," he said.

"I hate flying in coach," she clarified.

"Anything for Daddy's Little Girl," he said, studying her figure. "How about I trade it in for an abortion?"

True Stories as Bedtime Hyperbole

"Did he really say that?" Carly asked, sitting in Garnet's lap as her mom feathered her hair. She had had a hard time getting to sleep recently. Growing pains, Garnet supposed.

"He really did."

These stories helped Carly relax at night, when the street-lights flickered off. They were family fables. She had counted her share of sheep already.

"What does that even mean?"

"It means your grandfather didn't want you to be born," Garnet said.

"That's silly."

"I know it's silly – look how amazing you turned out."

Garnet could not be prouder. Carly was a happy Mozart at 9, learning piano, playing the organ at church. A prodigy, tickling the ivories. Robin, the more tomboyish of the two, was still figuring out her favorite things. She had loved picking yellow dandelions out of the yard, when they had a yard. When it used to rain.

"Mom, are you ok?" Carly asked.

Generally ok, yes. Specifically ok, never.

"I will be," Garnet whispered.

"Because I feel like I don't know you lately."

"Well, a good way to get to know me is to start asking questions."

"Okay," Carly said. "Where's your silver medal?"

"In your father's sock drawer."

Carly nodded, in approval.

"Okay. Then what's your favorite flower?"

"Guess," Garnet said.

The Stuff Dreams Are Made Of

"I just found out about the Maltese Falcon," Ty wrote in the subject line of his e-mail, as politely as he could. His ex-stepsister, Jodi, had the bird, and Ty thought this was the best way to get it back. "You know it was one of Dad's favorite things and among his favorite films. As I helped him through his successive cancers and his final week in the hospital he referenced how much he wished the statue was still in the family. When they dropped him off at Kennedy Hospital at Indio all he had with him with a duffel bag, some old clothes and a half-smoked pack of cigarettes. That's and one of his old billfolds is really all I have of his."

The very prospect of resuming contact with Jodi repelled Ty. He continued: "As the custodian of Arthur's legacy – and not just the closest to him, but really the only one who truly cared about and for him in his final years, through his homelessness and sobriety – I think it's appropriate that I have the bird. Of course there's so much more to discuss, family and such – a lot of the distance I keep, for reasons I know you can understand, to protect my family from your mother as much as possible. You and Stuart have always been terrific to me and you know we have no beef at all. Truth be told, I do have – and am working through – some residual bitterness about everyone's wholesale abandonment of Arthur, the overall absence of any condolences, the general disinterest in his well-being, so on. But it wasn't just his family, it was his friends and former associates who turned a blind eye.

This is clearly more than just about Arthur's ephemera. But I do like to think that if something of your dad or mom's, for example, came into my possession, I'd contact you on the presumption that you'd want an item of such sentimental and filial value returned.

At any rate, let me know whatever arrangement works best for you.

Best, Ty."

Two days later Ty received the following reply, not from Jodi but from her husband Stuart:

"Ty, it has come time for me to step in and pull Jodi from the middle of this situation. Here is what is going to happen with the Falcon going forward, per my decision. It has come to my attention that there is paperwork possibly adding some light to the authenticity of the falcon, and Yvonne is going to get that paperwork to us, should it turn up. If in fact there is any question to it being a genuine part of Hollywood movie history, then I will personally drive it to Los Angeles to an antiquities dealer that specializes in Hollywood artifacts and will help determine whether or not the Falcon is from the set. I have been in contact with the dealer, and we await the arrival of any paperwork before going forward. Please keep in mind I have put in many hours of research on it, and it does not look to be genuine at this point. However, if in fact it is, it will be placed with a museum of my choice, where it belongs, and the rest of the world to enjoy.

With that being said, I know Jodi appreciates the sentiment of you reaching out to her after all these years. I find your words to be very eloquently written, however, I also see the manipulation behind them as well. I also find the timing, and the request for an artifact and family heirloom that could potential hold a great monetary value, to be rather unethical, and with a very low degree of moral compass. We consider family to be a very sacred thing, and we consider you to be part of our family. Let it also be said, whether you choose to accept or not is largely irrelevant, that Arthur is part of her family as well. I will leave it at that, further discussion with you on that point will be moot. You have shown a rather large degree of disregard for your family here, for whatever reasons you find to be valid. Unfortunately with that decision comes consequences, and that consequence is I find no reason to separate the Falcon from our hands at this point. It was a gift from within the family, and it will stay as such if it does not find a home in a museum. Your disagreement with that decision will be unfortunate, I hope that one day, you will appreciate that it stayed within the family.

Please accept an open invitation to rejoin the family which you have chosen to forget. We will always be here with open arms. It truly does break your sister's heart that you feel the need to shield your family from your past."

Classic Stuart. Ty let this sink in for a minute, then sent off this missive:

"A few things: 1) the bird is a replica, and 2) just because you came into possession of something a few weeks ago doesn't mean it's yours. Please know that this does not belong to you and that I will not hesitate to engage a lawyer if you insist on its sole ownership. Also the tone of your letter was unnecessarily shitty. You never met Dad. You have no idea."

Ty's heart was beginning to accelerate. He was unaccustomed to this kind of conflict. Also he was lying: Arthur's Maltese was one of nine made from the same mold for the movie, though this bird never got any on-screen time.

Stuart nearly immediately replied:

"Unfortunately, yes, in the eyes of the law, an item passed from owner (Yvonne) to another person(s) (Jodi and I) does in fact, by law, show ownership, and that I can prove. Engage a lawyer if you must. Unless you have clearly signed paperwork from your father stating it is yours, or was willed to you, there is little in the eyes of the law that can be done. Until that day comes, it shall remain locked in a safe deposit box, and in the possession of the family that it always has been.

I don't pretend to know Arthur, not even in the least. You're absolutely correct in that I have no idea. However, thankfully I do know your sister, and her relationship with your father, and that is all that matters to me. You can cloud the life story all you wish, you can twist words to shine the light on you as the glorious person you are, if that is what you do to cherish his memory, I would never look to think otherwise. I have no dog in that fight. My intent is largely irrelevant, you know that. It's my actions that define who I am. And you have my decision. Do with it as you see fit, I never expected you to accept it."

Ty was steamed. "I wrote you a warm and honest letter," he wrote. "I truly did. You elected to respond callously and clumsily. I have a hard time buying your claim that the Maltese has so much sentimental meaning. You've really become attached to it over the past few weeks you've had it, I suppose. You claim it's a family heirloom and you're right, it is: for me.

As I said before – and I feel like I'm talking to a shoplifter or something – just because you have something doesn't mean it belongs to you. This whole business has upset me greatly, mostly because it has yet again shed light as to why I have protected my family from you and Yvonne. When are you both going to stop stealing from me? When? When will it stop? You'd better lawyer up, because I already have."

"There was nothing warm about you or your letter, Ty," Jodi replied herself, finally. "Stuart responded in my stead in an effort to protect ME from YOU. As you can see, that runs both ways. You find it necessary to protect your wife and he feels the same way. As to the rest of your delusional comments, I won't justify them with an answer. We are in this situation because of decisions you made. Deal with it.

"Jodi, look," Ty fired off. "The issue isn't 'yours versus mine.' I worry — and please be open-minded when I say this, I mean please hear this — is that you're seeing money on the brain where there isn't any. Fact: I know the guy who gave Arthur the bird. It's a sentimental artifact. Fact: you or Yvonne couldn't have cared less about — and I wager were not in contact with —Arthur for twenty years before his death. Fact: I was. Did Arthur collapse at and have to halt your wedding? What cancers did he have? Fact: you are now in possession of more than what I am in possession of Arthur's without caring for or about him. Fact: anyone who knew Arthur — including people who were present when he acquired the bird — would and have said they will attest to its belonging to me.

I respect you, I think you're a smart person, and you know at minimum this is a decision that includes me. It seems like if you're not willing to accept that then I will intervene with our lawyer — and I'm afraid that I'm not bluffing — and given that I have worked both at museums and appraisal studios, I hope it doesn't come to that. You will not successfully hide it or give it to a museum, I can guarantee you that now. Let's please find an amicable solution before we fight this out. You never cared for Arthur and all of this hurts even more dredging up memories of my caring for him alone and frankly I would fight harder for it given your attitude toward him as some cash-cow when he died with $42 and a half dozen cigarettes to his name."

"Ty," Jodi said, "it was never about you and I, I agree. I feel you underestimate the relationship between me and Arthur. The conversation is over, sorry. All contact from you in any form from this point will be noted and used in a possible harassment suit."

Ty couldn't win; he knew it. He also knew that his father didn't care about the bird; he merely liked it. Was he in it for the money, or for the memory of someone he only faintly liked, going to all the deathbed lengths for Arthur not out of love, but obligation? And why stress over it? Arthur would laugh all of this off, but Ty wasn't strong enough to let it go. He could only fume.

It occurred to Ty, weeks after he had let this set in, after he engaged a lawyer and proceeded to file an injunction against the bird's sale – all he could really do, legally – that this entire unfortunate episode dovetailed so strikingly with the plot of *The Maltese Falcon*. The movie was not always better than the book, and in Dashiell Hammett's case it was a dead heat.

Seventy-five years later, the bird, and copies thereof, was still claiming victims. Humphrey Bogart was right. The Maltese was, indeed, the stuff nightmares were made of.

Brutal Commute

He was delayed at Millbrae due to a pedestrian fatality, and texted his wife to let her know. *Some asshole jumped in front of the train in Atherton*, he said, and hit send, unaware that she was the asshole.

Football High School, Plano, TX

Beauty fades. Retired jerseys are forever.

Tonight's hero's morning alarm is a simpering chime, cueing sunrise, bench presses and parachute sprints. At lunchtime the D&D enthusiasts hunker in the library, pool their uncorrupted urine and finish his Trig homework.

He is tested weekly for both.

His future is bigger than his acne.

Tonight's hero can't see the scouts and the stadium is quiet as a cathedral. He says 'Student Body Left' and 'Om-a-ha' and '37 Fly Sweep.' Beyond this he has no vocabulary, or a need for one.

Tonight's hero will be incapable of confining his life to the sidelines.

At 41, a decade out of the game and thrice concussed – but immortalized in video games, and that was the objective – tonight's hero will toggle around his old glory, hitting A to throw and B to play-fake, taunting in the end zone as he scores a virtual TD against another highly touted hero from whom he'd just that afternoon bought a good used Chevy Impala, ~289,000 miles, just shy of the record.

Open Concept

Ursula Soto-Coslett was 27 years old, 4'11," 185 lbs. Her life was starved yet fable-like. She lived in Huntington, New York, a five-minute walk from the Long Island Rail Road. As a Northern Californian, Ursula pronounced it as one word, *LIRR*, which rolled off her tongue unlike the transit systems back home in the Bay Area. All the other New Yorkers she knew, even those transplanted from the Midwest, spelled it out to the letter.

From coast to coast, BART to LIRR, the early morning commuters read or slept silently, mouths open. The LIRR ran through towns named Belmont, Amityville, the fuselage smelling like feet, mangoes. It was an hour-long trip into Manhattan on LIRR, then downtown to Pace University, where Ursula recruited mathematicians into the university's graduate program. The job paid $55,000 a year when her counterparts at Stanford made $70,000, with more attainable metrics and infinitely less to do. Working in higher education had always been her principal goal, and there were compensations that would keep her employed there, maybe not rising up through the administrative ranks as she'd dreamed but in the ranks nonetheless. For instance, Pace incentivized its employees to adopt children, with a $5,000 allowance to offset most of the fees.

Maternity leave, in contrast, was much less lucrative.

Ursula was an adoptee. She didn't know her parents and didn't want to. Her husband, Cahn, had bought her a DNA test as a wedding present, in lieu of a honeymoon. They had been married at City Hall without much fanfare and no rings to exchange, and afterwards they celebrated by walking the Brooklyn Bridge and toasting with pints of Yuengling at Grimaldi's. She had thought she was a full-blooded Latina – all of her friends knew her as such, it explained her fieriness and distemper – but when the blood panel came back reading 55 percent Irish and 45 percent Guatemalan, Ursula was not disconsolate. Instead, it seemed fitting. It made sense. She liked Guinness. She liked fried plantains.

Her shortness was not a hindrance. There was no clinical term for her height – she was neither a 'dwarf' nor even a 'short person' – and she made up for it by wearing four-inch heels, with a different cardigan for every day of the week. She was not a workaholic but she was efficient and enthusiastic. In no time she was employee-of-the-month at Pace, a campus-wide honor that won her a $50 gift card to Red Lobster. It was her thoughtfulness, her thinking outside the box that endeared her to her colleagues. She stalked her students on the Internet and kept an updated spreadsheet of their interests and birthdays. She got them luggage tags as graduation gifts. Gifts were her love language, as were baked goods.

In Spring 2013 Ursula and Cahn opened up their marriage. Spring became summer, and as New Yorkers are wont to do, Ursula bitched about the choking, dense Long Island heat to her parents. She began drinking cheap merlot out of frosted mugs from Dollar Tree in the evenings, deep in a rocking chair that she braced with her calves, arriving at so many epiphanies that it was hard for her to keep track. She thought about the termite queens who couldn't achieve sexual fulfillment or shed their wings without first taking flight, just once. On board game nights with friends she spelled out *polyamory* with Scrabble tiles.

Her first flight was someone from her past whose name she had come across in a gossip magazine, whose name she swore to protect because he had so much more to lose if he was found out. By some miracle Lansing's phone number was the same as it was in high school and if it wasn't for all the 4's in it she's have forgotten it.

It started out innocently, PG. Lansing was happily married also, and in a similar situation as Ursula without the explicit openness. He and his bride had a rule that governed casual hookups only, and like Ursula, he hadn't yet exercised his right, though his wife had, with a Canadian performer in Las Vegas, *at Circus Circus, of all places,* he said.

It was Lansing, not Lance. Never Lance. Whenever Ursula saw his name on her phone she exclaimed in little squeals and giggles. She emoted. *I emoji you,* she told him, which was approximately equal to love. She sent him gifts to his workplace – slate coasters from a boutique in Red Hook, a wine key, fancy chocolates made with saffron and pepper. In turn he bought her a crystal goblet from Kate Spade – her favorite brand, KS, her two favorite words – and a book of vegan recipes because, as he remembered her saying when they were dating in high school –

In our future life together you will not eat meat. You will not smoke. Both of which Lansing did as an adult, habitually, daily.

It was why she and Lansing didn't work out as teenagers. Ursula was an ultimatum person. In Cahn she had met her perfect match. Lansing avoided becoming a wedge between them, and he praised the Lord (or Whomever, because he didn't really care for the Afterlife, but he thanked the Lord first, to cover all of his bases) Who created Nevada and Nebraska and all the states between he and Ursula, which were difficult for him to traverse because he was terrible on planes, because he flew horribly and refused to medicate himself in-flight. In this sense he was anomalous, just as Ursula had remembered him: Lansing wore broken watches that worked but couldn't be read. Lansing wore his jeans inside-out. Lansing never ditched 4th period. Lansing couldn't fly.

If it felt wrong at any point Ursula would have put a halt to it. Still, she had to get creative to hide Lansing from Cahn, because she was developing potent, old feelings for him. Lansing was not even in her phone as Lansing Peobles but as Abraham Yee, an old co-worker of hers who, as she put it to her husband, was running roughshod over all of the single men in Chelsea. She had bought herself the Kate Spade goblet, she told Cahn, splurging on herself for once.

Ursula was proud of the elaborateness of her lies. Lansing was white. They were white lies.

One afternoon, Lansing said he was so overdue for a visit to New York that he'd be there in two weeks, if that was okay with her, and that if she could take a day off he'd show her around the Brooklyn he knew.

No pressure, he said.

The morning of his arrival into Kennedy, Ursula got her period. The weather was variable, it was October, the changing leaves excited her but when the wind kicked up at Grand Army Plaza she grew irritable that Lansing wasn't doing a better job of shielding her from it. They lunched on a shared plate of braised kale and lentil salad outside of the Brooklyn Museum. Lansing talked about how his father and uncle and Huell Howser had passed away within months of one another, and how he had a healthy, almost casual view on death, and how he loved her, really truly. They walked everywhere – 20,000 steps according to her fitness tracker –, from bar to bar, holding hands. She told him she'd leave Cahn if he only said the word.

Who does this, she said, over and over again. *Who?*

I would leave her, Lansing said. *I will and I would.*

They were at the Gowanus Yacht Club, in Carroll Gardens. She was on her fifth High Life.

It won't work, she said. *I'm not seventeen anymore.*

What time is it?

What's time, she said. *I've forgotten.*

Ursula.

Don't, she said.

Let me walk you back to your train.

That was it. At Atlantic Terminal she tried to remember the old him, the teenage Lansing, years before his accidental viral fame, the kid who had bleached his hair and proposed to her at Prom, and how happy she was to tell him *No*. As her train rolled into Jamaica Station the day's drinking finally hit her. She forgot how much she had consumed, how drunk Lansing had made her, how she'd gone drink for drink with this man who was notorious for his intake. She fell asleep in a tunnel – just a cat-nap – and awoke not in Huntington but in Babylon, an extra hour deep in the Hamptons, the outer limits of LIRR, and next to her a stranger she didn't know who had his hand up her dress. She bolted up and out of the train and when she checked it her mobile battery was dead and the man followed her off the platform to a pay-phone.

I have mace, she screamed.

Then she called Cahn collect and took an $80 ride home in an unmarked livery, not humiliated, but for the first time, not confused by men.

It was money she did not have.

No Wins

Gregory Buonnatale was only somewhat aware that the methuselah of champagne he ordered up from Calimesa Country Club's wine cellar – *Guy Larmandier*, blanc et noir, NV – to guzzle and lap out of the silver Club Championship trophy he had won just a few hours earlier – finishing 36 holes in 2 under par, a new record for members over 55 – probably cost more than the trophy had itself, silver having plunged $4 per ounce that morning on the commodities market as he attended to one of his daughter's nose-bleeds. This did not diminish Greg's enthusiasm as he wiped the dust out of the inside of the trophy with the side of his palm, running his finger along the faceplate where his name would soon be etched. There had not before been an opportunity or excuse for such indulgence. In fact Greg had never so much as bought a round of drinks for any of the members, most of them his friends and clients, and furthermore he did not know that he would never do so again: after attempting to drive home and instead steering his cherry-red Mazda Miata through a weave of spruce trees and onto the 9th green, yelling 'I AM SIMBA!' repeatedly into the cloudless September air and in full view of so many stars, towed away with his parking brake and hazards on, his golf and tennis privileges revoked by the club's Rules Committee, though not unanimously.

The episode would have passed with nominal scandal or damage, but it was one of the high school caddies moonlighting at the course for the summer, as a source on deep background, who outed Greg in the weekly local paper, having been spurned by his daughter, Laurie, at Homecoming *and* Prom, unaware that her proboscal membranes were thinner than most, obliging her to spend the better part of school dances in a bathroom stall crying with a tampon stanching the flood from her nose. It was almost more pleasing to the boy that revenge had come to him purely by accident. The headline in the paper that week, in garish 48-point font, pegged Greg as Calimesa's 'Lion King' and by some editorial sleight-of-hand managed to isolate a quote from a certain internal and confidential report the Rules Committee had drafted that also pretty much summed up what everyone in town felt:

'If only Buonnatale had cheated, instead of swerved.'

Traditional Marriages

I

At Coach Pierce's prompting his high school sprinters entered their lanes. Gravelly footfalls, raillery in the blocks. The glandular thrills of young track and field.

Superstitiously, Pierce touched one toe of his cleat across the other. It was the summer solstice, the sunlight up late. Smog so thick he hadn't seen the mountains for weeks.

He could still outrun everyone, glancing back as he kicked past the seniors. The squad was conditioning for the autumn meets. They were lazy and their hearts weren't in it.

He waited at the finish line, the starter's pistol tucked in his shorts, looking them in the eyes as they each came in.

Showers were hurdles. They fogged his mind. He was at 29 where he thought he'd be at 24: behind his own curve. His hamstrings trembled, lukewarm in the old pipes. Periodic cold blasts.

His team was slow. The boredom hurt. To them, winning was abstract.

Pierce lathered in the wet hot and assigned all the fault to himself. The hard years he knew were ahead were finally here.

II

Jaundiced pages from mildewed books as pocket squares, day-old carnations in his lapels: Leopold Christian was a millionaire if he counted the house and the Cadillacs. He had failed epically before this new oil company venture of his. He treated every business negotiation like it was Appomattox, and he was U.S. Grant.

Pierce, his eldest son, went through life thinking it would never rain on him. Pierce had untold abilities and inexhaustible potential. It all came to him easily. He was in the clouds, unsinkable. Anything he wanted landed in his lap, just as Leo had orchestrated it.

III

A convertible squealed up to the pumps, lurching forward as the engine stalled. Pierce parted the office blinds. Its driver looked around arrestingly, as if she had never pumped fuel before. As if she only knew how to stop traffic.

Her cluelessness was tactical. It was her bait.

Pierce went to her, shabbily in seersucker, strolling to the islands. He didn't want to excite or frighten her ... you know how it is when someone handsome comes into your field of vision.

She was impressed by his deftness and before he could even ask, she wrote her phone number into a slick of grime caked on the pump.

"Who should I ask for?"

"Mina Averill," she said.

He opened her door, and closed it behind her. Mina revved the engine. Chivalry never missed.

IV

"Hello, may I speak to Mina? Is this Mr. Averill? Yes, sir. Pierce Christian speaking."

He pictured Mina's father in Hawaiian wear, croissant flakes on his trousers, reading the racing form in the wicker rocker on the porch, off its track. Pierce hoped he was wrong, but he had an unfortunate knack of reading people over the phone.

"She's indisposed? Please tell her I called. Yes, that's my father's company. Yes, I can't wait to meet you too."

Hanging up the receiver, Pierce thought of this line: *the American attention span is a short, ignorant fuse.*

V

Mina got carsick whenever she wasn't driving. Migraine blurs: tightly closing her eyes and opening them to the flood of light. She saw auras and stars and the static of radio chatter.

First date. Pierce thought it would not impress her to drop names or throw money around. He drove her to Cozzo's Rib, where the patrons wore bibs instead of neckties. The waiters loitered impassively. Their teeth like pearls. Seated old people, tipping poorly.

Pierce ordered for the both of them. Mina dunked a baguette into olive oil.

"My first meal of the day," she said.

She felt for Pierce's leg and couldn't find it. It occurred to her that she might be too old to flirt under the table.

With Mina, Pierce tried to imagine, for he had never seen it, his parents madly in love.

A smattering of light applause and the house music at Cozzo's started up, mute and bourgeois. She snickered at the musicians' clothes.

"Don't laugh," Pierce said. "This song made everyone cry forty years ago."

Mina laughed easily. She was a good kid with an enchanted life, practicing autographs of her screen-names-to-be, her navel studded with zirconium. Saying, she would rather have a piercing she regretted than have none.

Pierce did several things unselfconsciously and with inordinate grace. Eating wasn't one of them. Silverware crashed and chimed in his hands. He felt heroic because he left large tips.

For Mina, it was her Jesus complex. She wanted a man like his, with problems.

VI

Leo Christian's twenties had been a rolling blackout, while his thirties roared. Into his late sixties he had worked arduous hours, as if he had all the time in the world, his mental faculties slowly degrading. He could hear his mind snapping its fingers. It wasn't death he feared, it was not knowing the time and day, not knowing the gradient of his decline.

He had been occasioned lately to murderous kindnesses, atonements for the days when he had nothing, when he brushed off encumbrances and mistresses, inviting them to scratch on the chain-mail of his wristwatch band, to drink free on his tab. ("*Mr. Christian* does *have a tab open, doesn't he?*") When he talked for a living. Made his living talking. His gift of random recall. A wallet stacked with tarot-card-size family portraits. He divulged nothing, especially emotions.

His wife of forty years, Eloise, knew his mood from the way her shuffling about the house rattled him. Married this long and sleeping on opposite sides of the house. Leo's anger was a rolling boil: he talked in profit margins, a cacophony of commerce. He was vulgar and jonquil with Eloise, a surly gossip of a grown woman.

It was Pierce who bailed Leo out the week he was made honorary sheriff and, shoving the token badge in the airport cops' faces, caught trying to carry a gun onto a plane to Phoenix.

Eloise's skin was saran-thin, a protrusion of veins, a face dry and pocked from years of treatments and creams. Most nights ended with her wedging Leo's boots off with shoehorns and guessing the color of Vanna White's dress, as Leo gnawed on a stub of cigar and Eloise knit. It made her approximately happy, just having Leo around to complain to, or about. How she could never find a decent parking space downtown. About her pathetic allowance.

Leo was old. It was inevitable. He made noises getting out of chairs. He ate prunes.

VII
On their second date, Mina drank two martinis and threw up on Pierce's shoes.

VIII
Sometimes there was a look in her eyes. Pierce couldn't tell if Mina wanted a dog or a child, his own cosmic aesthetic pure chaos.

She wanted to be the architect of his life. When she closed her eyes she didn't see darkness or neon curlicues: she saw herself and Pierce in fifty years as old people frolicking.

His nickname for her was a Ralston-brand breakfast cereal – Crazy Cow – because she was *so* wholesome.

IX
Pierce started shaving for her. The sensation of running a lawn-mower over his face.

Paintings wrinkle. Epitaphs wither. On most graves the names aren't even legible.

"I saw this couple on a bench yesterday," she said. "He was smoking a big cigar. She was feeding birds. You never saw two people so happy." This was her goal.

Standing in her socks on the tile in their vestibule, Mina did little twirls, checking her profile in the mirror, getting up close to look at her pores. An old mirror, the nickel decaying.

X
He ambushed her by placing the engagement ring on the table, next to her Earl Grey. He saw the glint of her crying and surprise.

"You have to say something!"

"The diamond says it all," Pierce said.

"Say it."

"I'd be delighted if you– "

"Delighted?," she said. "Me too."

A diamond as large as Gibraltar. He raised her left arm. Mouths fell in excitement. Dictators were toppled.

XI

Eloise had hated him so much for so long, she couldn't imagine life without him.

In his tepid, nightly bath, Leo pawed at his scalp. He had started business late in life and reaped the customary returns: a family that resented him, a son he didn't recognize, faded mornings, a pocketbook of mistresses, expense reports he couldn't account for. The miracle was what it did to his heart: hardening it. Lionhearted. The new fibrillation of its cadence. When he wrote out dicta he could never spell *rhythm*, or *marriage*, and he couldn't make work what he couldn't spell.

Leo heard a knock on the bathroom door. He was afraid Eloise might throw a toaster in the tub. But no, she only wanted to say hello, this time.

XII

Pierce was awed by her inborn, unmutable exuberance. They stayed up until 3 a.m., laying still and flat on the trampoline in their front yard to watch the stars flicker and the flights course by overhead. The heavens disappointed Mina, but she never did say it out loud, only hinted, her tongue clicking in displeasure. So skillful was she at onomatopoeias.

1985 was a year of two wonderful things: Pierce turned thirty and Mina read Julio Cortazar. She had a thing for saviors and the portraits in her mind were of a rotogravure of Pierce at rest, loitering on the couch in his dud clothes, sleeping in on Sundays well past noon. She, the little woman slaving happily in the kitchen, two hours out of every day reserved for cleaning or making pasta and sauce from scratch.

The future. She already had the color of the nursery picked out, with twenty names for girls and none for boys.

"Don't you worry?" she asked Pierce.

"About what?"

"Our kids bicycling on a busy street."

"I did it all the time."

"You can't just let the kids run loose."

"Why not? Let them get into a little trouble."

"What if they're killed?"

"Seriously?"

"I'll blame you if anything happens," she said. "What's your position on helmets?"

That year he saw his first dandruff. He contemplated making a change, perhaps to decaf coffee, or menthol cigarettes.

XIII

Pierce loved Los Angeles and she didn't. They found a good steak restaurant and drank to the years, opening finer wines as the meal went on, superlative vintages.

"What am I tasting?" Mina asked the sommelier.

"I don't know, ma'am," he replied. "I've never been in your mouth."

XIV

Eloise had heard of a store in Cucamonga that sold books by the yard. Mina might like that.

Bookstores intimidated her. The shelves were a maze. The dust choked her up. She coughed. A clerk peered down from a ladder.

"Can you recommend a novel for my daughter-in-law?"

"I can recommend some titles. How about John Steinbeck?"

He was so high up. Mina didn't want to trouble him.

"Just give me his newest release," she said.

XV

"How's married life?" Leo asked Pierce.

"As you well know, it's like cramming one year of sex into ten years," his son joked.

XVI

One night, Mina caught Pierce thinning out a line of cocaine, after a heavy dinner he had hardly touched.

"Just a small one," he said. "As a digestif."

XVII

"You know what they told me when I left Byrn Mawr?" Mina told Pierce. "'*Only our failures marry.*'"

When Pierce imagined all-girls' schools, he pictured twenty women sharing one urinal.

XVIII

Leo lost his color first, then his weight, once so leathery and robust. Living without an obituary. After all, death doesn't need facing, because it's not lived through, in the same way that one never leaves a fraternity, even in death. One only changes chapters.

Next to his bed was a Bible, which he never got around to reading. He didn't want to burden Eloise with the funeral arrangements, but at her age she had one purpose, and for better or worse, Leo was it. There was a folder in his study, he instructed her, a playbook for taking care of his affairs – from funeral arrangements to insurance policies – on which he had written simply '*Answers*.'

All this macabre talk unnerved Eloise. She got Pierce on the phone and put it to Leo's ear.

"Your father moved his bowels twice today," she told Pierce.

"I might as well have died at Guadalcanal," Leo said.

Eloise smiled. "You weren't in the Pacific theatre, remember?"

Pierce wrongly thought the old man would plug away at his cancer like Joe Frazier, wearing it down.

Later, when the mortician courteously asked Eloise if she would like to press the shirt Leo was to be buried in, she declined.

Forty years of starching his shirts. She'd had enough.

XVIII

The day Mina took back her maiden name, she threw a pair of never-used tennis shoes over some telephone wires on her block.

According to Pierce, it took her eleven tries.

XIX

She was not around for her son's fourth Christmas, when Wells got a laser tag set. He tore open the packaging, and frowned. It was the wrong set, apparently.

"Stupid Santa!" Wells pouted.

Pierce, his proud lonely papa, laughed, getting it all on the camcorder.

XX

"You have her facial features," Pierce told Wells during their weekly telephone date. *"You're strange like her. Before you were born we visited a Native American artifacts gallery somewhere in Santa Monica. Your mother saw a pair of high-top moccasins made in 1889. This place is like a museum, mind you. She went wild and ran up to the proprietor. 'The price is fine,' she told him, 'but do you have these in a size six?'"*

XXI

Wells' genes were like a deformity he didn't learn about until adulthood. His family history wasn't easy piecing together, but fortunately no-one had any interest in making themselves out to be the hero. Everyone was guilty.

He had just returned from Las Vegas. A colleague had had his bachelor party at the Quad, which used to be the Imperial Palace, which used to be plain dry, clean desert. The boys spent the days poolside with margaritas. Wells couldn't wait to leave. He motioned for a porter to bring a phone.

"I hope you're not calling your ex," a friend counseled.

He did. Somehow he remembered the sequence. She answered like he knew she would.

"Cindy, it's Wells."

He heard her draw a breath: a knife plunged into the receiver.

"Wells. Your timing is impeccable," she said. "I'm giving birth tomorrow."

He needn't worry. It wasn't his.

XXII

Mina checked the weather before work. She talked to herself about her errands and the order in which she would run them. After work she walked home from the farmer's market with a bat of Brussels sprouts over her shoulder.

As if she was going to knock dinner out of the park.

XXIII

Mina spied a man tramping through the unmown roughage in her yard. She didn't recognize him: his hair was matted and in his eyes, beastly. He looked thoroughly disreputable.

She considered drawing the blinds. He might be a collector for the local utility.

Wells rang the bell, and when it didn't work, he knocked on the screen. Mina summoned the courage the answer. She had her checkbook in hand.

"Excuse me, ma'am. Does a Mina live here?" Wells straightened up. "I don't have her new last name."

XXIV

Her house was musty and eclectically furnished. A light bulb in a birdcage. Commemorative plates with gilded bald eagles.

She was nearing fifty. Her index finger was bandaged. She had hurt herself on a mandolin, cooking. The Band-Aid was frayed and bloodied.

The joy of children was supposed to move her. It didn't. It was supposed to compel her to responsibility and didn't.

She remembered she had bathed Wells clumsily, in the kitchen sink with the little spray gun meant for rinsing plates, as if he was a pet.

"You're taller than your father," she said.

Mina wanted to direct his attention to the AA pledge on the wall. There was so much to say. But her little girl walked in with her bicycle, dropped it on the floor, and interrupted with slamming drawers.

XXV

"Becky, this is Wells."

She reached out a hand. "Hello. You're from around here?"

"No, California."

"Hollywood? What movies are you in?"

Wells laughed.

"Mom, I'm going to watch a show."

Becky went into the next room. One of those console TVs, with the knobs.

"Where's her father?" Wells asked.

"I don't know," Mina said. "He sold encyclopedias."

"I bet she's already had her first cigarette," Wells said.

XXVI

She had a fast gait. On the way to the nearby creamery Wells bent over in the street and picked up a coin. It was heads. He showed it to her.

"You don't have to pick up every lucky penny you find," Mina said. "Then again, you *were* born on Friday the 13th."

They sat across from one another and shared a malted. Half chocolate, half pistachio. Wells hadn't had his share, but Mina poured herself what was left in the silver mug.

"I teach for a living."

"Great," she said.

Wells shifted, uncomfortably.

"Look, I want your name off of my birth certificate."

"What?"

"Your name. Having you removed."

"But you can't. What would it say?"

"Nothing," Wells said. "It would say nothing. Which is exactly how it happened."

"You didn't come all this way to tell me that. Look, I have to do something tonight," Mina said. "I don't know what your plans are. Would you stay with Becky for an hour?"

XXVII

Mina was gone for six. It grew dark. Becky watched four shows and made Wells dinner. Macaroni in a box. She even set out the TV trays.

"Who are you really?"

Wells shrugged. He wasn't an old friend. He wasn't just passing through.

"I'm recruiting for a college I work for. What grade are you in?" he asked.

She was engrossed in her show.

"Do you get good grades?"

Rapt by the animation.

"Do they even give grades at your school?"

It was a circus show.

"When I was your age I watched this too," Wells said.

"Where was your dad?"

"Working."

"Where was your mom?"

"I don't know," he said, softly.

"You should have tried out for sports," Becca said.

"Think so? Which ones?"

"Bowling," she said.

"I never asked to."

"Not even kickball?"

"Not even," Wells said.

When he heard the front door finally latch and unlatch, he stood up quickly and flicked off the tube.

"I have to leave soon. I'm leaving my number and my California address on the fridge. We can be pen pals."

"What's that?"

"That's where we write letters to one another."

"I guess I would just call you," Becca said. "Or e-mail."

XXVIII

Wells sent Becky a fountain pen, stationery and some stamps. They might soon be artifacts in her closet, but at least the stamps wouldn't lose their value.

XXIX

No one knew – not even her landlord – that the towel rack near the tub in Mina's house was heated by an electrical current at a low voltage. It was a feature the previous general contractor had installed without either telling anyone, or anyone remembering.

One night after soccer practice Becky grabbed hold of it to brace herself getting out of the tub. Her elbow had a large bruise, where the electricity somehow escaped. The hospital bill exceeded $4,000, and the day it arrived in the mail Mina told Becky how much she loved her and how sorry she was. That afternoon she took a suitcase with her to the grocery store. At dinnertime Becca made herself a can of O's, and two days later, called Wells from a nearby police station.

He decided she didn't need to hear the whole saga. What she needed to hear was:

Yes, I'll get you a plane ticket.

No, I'm not going to wire you money.

No, a missing person's report won't help.

Yes, you're big enough to call a cab to the airport.

You'll Like Tacoma

There is a Karpeles Historical Documents Library down the street from us. Sam is the one employee. Admission is free. In the morning Sam takes the dozen or so priceless papers out of the safe. At night he puts them back in.

Last week Sam broke Einstein's journals. The binding shattered. I helped him glue them back together.

24 left. 31 right. 20 left.

Any Questions?

We are leaving Sunday early in the morning. We have a lock box. There is a gate door on the left side of our house. Enter. As soon as you enter, the lock box is attached. You will see it when you enter the gate on your left.

1219 is the code. Take the key and get in the house.

Cocoa and Maya will bark at first but they will be fine. Please let them out.

Dogs: We change their water every day. We just give them the water from the faucet. We feed them once a day. There are treats on the counter in the kitchen. You can give them a treat here and there.

Home: We have a guest bedroom. It is upstairs, first room on the right. Everything is clean. We had a housekeeper come and no one has used the room since. Make that your room. I will try to clean up a bit. I store all my stuff in there.

Bathroom: We have a bathroom downstairs and you guys can use the one in the hallway. I will leave your room and both bathrooms open for you guys.

Pots and Pans/Kitchen: Feel free to use what we have at home. We don't have groceries.

We are planning to fly back June 7th. Please call my mother-in-law and give her the dogs and lock all doors when you guys leave. 766-548-2297. Our trip schedule may change so please keep communication with Helen. She will know our plans.

Dogs: If you guys can pick up poop in the backyard once a week, that would be great.

Cocoa and Maya love to walk if you guys want to take them. There is a park nearby. Their harness and leash is in the garage by the work table. See a white basket on top with their stuff. Maya's pink harness is by my shoes.

They would appreciate a shower every 2 weeks. We just washed them.

I stopped our mail.

Make yourself at home.

No shoes in the house.

Any questions?